Eustace Clare Grenville Murray

Strange Tales

Eustace Clare Grenville Murray

Strange Tales

ISBN/EAN: 9783337377731

Printed in Europe, USA, Canada, Australia, Japan

Cover: Foto ©Andreas Hilbeck / pixelio.de

More available books at **www.hansebooks.com**

COLLECTION

OF

BRITISH AUTHORS

TAUCHNITZ EDITION.

VOL. 1793.

STRANGE TALES BY E. C. GRENVILLE: MURRAY.

IN ONE VOLUME.

TAUCHNITZ EDITION.

By the same Author,

STRANGE TALES.

BY

E. C. GRENVILLE: MURRAY,

AUTHOR OF "THE RUSSIANS OF TO-DAY," ETC.

COPYRIGHT EDITION.

"Saturnalitias mittimus, ecce nuces."

L E I P Z I G

B E R N H A R D   T A U C H N I T Z

1878.

The Right of Translation is reserved.

TO

GEORGE AUGUSTUS SALA Esq.

THE EMINENT JOURNALIST, AND MAN OF LETTERS,
WHOSE CONVERSATION IS AS VARIED AND BRILLIANT,
AS HIS WRITINGS ARE INSTRUCTIVE AND DELIGHTFUL,
THIS BOOK IS INSCRIBED, FOR AN ACT OF HOMAGE
TO HIS WIT AND GENIUS.

CONTENTS.

8 CONTENTS.

STRANGE TALES.

No. 1.—True Love.

I REMEMBER the day, though nobody else does, when I cleared a ditch twenty feet wide, or less. Things were no cheaper that year than they usually are, but I saw a man go into a roadside inn and ask for pickled-salmon, a gooseberry tart, and some cider if they had any. They hadn't any, and I said claret would do as well, since he was so good as to invite me. He was a mournful stranger, and when I had seated myself by his side at once waxed confidential exclaiming:—

"Her hair was brown, and fell in ripples to her "waist, and if her uncle had consented to our "marriage we should have been eating ices this "evening in the Café Florian at Venice, revelling "in the third week of our honeymoon. But he "was of sordid soul, not above the petty gains of "trade, and I think he wanted to get into Parlia-"ment, judging by the way in which he hocussed

"the population. She was no better, and fanned me
"into fighting with an adjutant, who pitched me into
"a piece of ornamental water legs first. The next
"man was a Chamber Counsel, and there was no-
"thing left of him but his gloves, for we had it out
"among the rhododendrons after supper. The third
"fellow clapped my hat over my ears and eyes, and
"shot me down the staircase on to the mat at the
"bottom—I never saw anything like it. If you've
"been in love you know how one remembers those
"things, and I had less reason than anybody else to
"forget them, for the first time I set eyes on that
"girl I vowed she was too good for any but me. At
"the bazaar they held for the orphan baboons she
"kept a stall, and sold a piece of Swiss-roll for five
"pounds to a man on the Stock Exchange. I said,
"'Give me two pieces of that Swiss-roll'; and I don't
"envy that stockbroker's feelings as she put them
"on a plate for me and said, 'How greedy you have
"become!—here's a spoon to eat with.' 'Total, two
"spoons,' observed the stockbroker; 'but he won't
"eat, he means to wear them next his heart,' and she
"laughed till the jelly glasses jingled. You've been
"to the Star and Garter, and know the curve of the
"river with the red boat-house standing on the eyot
"in the middle. As we were loitering on the hotel
"terrace waiting for dinner on another occasion I

"ejaculated, 'That Thames is like you; it babbles
"and babbles and ripples away out of sight.' This
"was because she had slipped off, thinking to join
"the other ladies, and if you had seen them round
"the table with their silk dresses of all colours you'd
"have thought the scene was exciting enough with-
"out there needing to be so much cayenne in the
"whitebait. I tell you that's the happiest day but
"one I ever spent in my life, for they made me
"drive the drag home, and I knocked over a sign-
"post on Barnes Common and mistook the aque-
"duct at Putney for the bridge. My happiest day of
"all, however, was the Cup-day at Ascot. When we
"reached the King's statue at the top of the Long
"Walk I thought we had only just left the White
"Hart, and shouted to the postillions not to be in
"such a hurry. A gipsy sold us a racing-card, and
"a smaller one clung behind and cut down our
"hamper with his knife. She exclaimed, 'I'll bet six
"dozen pairs of gloves against the horse who comes
"in last,' and as soon as I had answered 'Done,' I
"noticed our hamper was gone. I scrambled down,
"and chased the gipsies as far as the rabbit warren.
"The conies bounded ahead of me like cricket-balls
"by twos and threes. I had a fight, and pelted
"back, waving my hat, and with the hamper; but
"robbed of my watch, which they had taken in ex-

"change, as I found out later. She clapped her
"hands though, and said I deserved the Cup all to
"myself; and by-and-by, when the last horse in the
"race ran in at the tail, I cried, 'That's six dozen I
"owe you.'   'Yes,' said she; 'two dozen of gray,
"two of lemon, and two of white—six-and-a-quarter
"size, with three buttons.'   Don't ever suppose I'd
"have exchanged our luncheon on that course for
"all Nasreddin's diamonds.   Her uncle had got into
"the enclosure, and was saying to a Parliamentary
"agent with a head like a turnip, 'My principles are
"those of a Cheap Government.'   'Come and have
"some champagne,' I interrupted; and he sang out
"with a sigh, 'I daresay you've heard the bad news
"—that stockbroker has broken his head.'   'I'm glad
"to learn he'd a head to break,' was my sensible
"answer.   Only this bad news was too good to be
"true, for it proved to be another stockbroker, and
"the one who had bought the Swiss roll turned up
"the very next evening, grinning like a pole-cat.   I
"knew he wasn't the man to break his neck to please
"me.   He had a whiskered face like a sunflower,
"and no more soul than a saucepan.   All the men
"who have ever thwarted me have been like that,
"and I have not a good word to say for one of them.
"No, not I, and it must always be so as long as the
"debased philosophy of a mercenary age makes light

"of all but tangible dross. I have palaces in my
"brain grander than that stockbroker ever lived in,
"and riches in fancy that would beggar Capel Court.
"But Soul is nowhere in the trial-heat with Cash,
"and limps in the hindmost like a roarer. That's
"how it is, you there, whatever your name is." The
stranger flourished his fork over his head, dropped
it, and glared at me. "Don't be downhearted," I
remarked, "and let us have the gooseberry tart in."

He helped himself largely, and went rambling
on as follows:—"That stockbroker invited them all
"to see him shoot pigeons with a breech-loader, at
"which sport he was no great gun; and the next
"day we played against each other in a cricket
"match at Lord's, and I was set bowling at the Pa-
"vilion end. I whistled a round-hander straight at
"his legs; he drove it back and knocked me down
"like a ninepin. They carried me in, and said they
"hoped it didn't hurt. I said it did, and the match
"proceeded without me, he making a hundred 'not
"out,' which was in the *Times* next day. The same
"evening, after I had dined off some gruel, I put a
"plaister over my eye and went to the opera. She
"was in a grand tier box with her uncle behind her,
"and a second Parliamentary agent with ears like
"jug-handles. I heard the uncle say as the box-
"keeper opened the door for me, 'I'm for the prin-

"ciples of a Cheap Government;' and the agent an-
"swered, 'There's nothing like it.' She turned round
"rustling with her blue dress, fan, pearls, flowers,
"and golden hair, and uttered a half-scream. 'What-
"ever have you been doing with your eye?' And I
"replied, 'It's somebody else that's been doing it,
"not I!' Then I sat down beside her and talked to
"her about the destinies of future ages and the plea-
"sures of imagination, things which women love to
"hear about, and we listened to Mozart's music.
"Where did you ever hear anything like that minuet
"in 'Don Giovanni?' The people in the stalls all
"swayed about as if they were being shampooed,
"and I saw that stockbroker clap his hands until his
"gloves must have cracked. I watched him with
"attention at the scene where Don Juan disappears
"in the flames, and I said to her grimly, 'Many's the
"stockbroker that must have gone down in that way.'
"I don't think she relished the remark, for presently
"we met the stockbroker on the staircase, and she
"held out her hand to him quite sweetly. This is a
"trick with women, and it makes me grind my teeth
"to madness. He observed to me, 'I'm really un-
"commonly sorry for that crack you got; if I had
"had time to think I should have hit another way.'
"I rejoined, 'You really can't be more sorry than I
"am; and if I had had time to think I should have

"got out of the light.' The truth is there was no
"love lost between us. He couldn't have been more
"distasteful to me if he'd been tarred and feathered,
"though I fancy I should have liked him better in
"that dress than in any other. We played two
"rubbers in company at the club, and he won six
"pounds three shillings of me—enough to pay him
"a steerage passage to New York, as I significantly
"hinted. But he has never taken my hint, and I
"made up my mind that I would be beforehand
"with him the next morning in speaking to her
"uncle. So I was there by noon, and I found him
"closeted with a third agent, who had a white hat,
"and to whom he said, 'I am fully resolved to sup-
"port a Cheap Government;' and the agent replied,
"'There's nothing beats it.' Both looked up as I
"entered, and I hurried to the point at once by ex-
"claiming, 'I've come to ask leave to pay my court
"to your niece, as I've been doing for the past
"twelvemonth. My income is smaller than my ge-
"nius, and my debts may be more than my credit.
"But you see me as I stand, imbued with unsullied
"principles, and if you make handsome settlements
"we can be married next month, and go on a tour
"to Italy, which I've never visited.' It was three
"parts of a minute before he answered, and I then
"gauged for the first time to what depths of im-

"becility the teachings of a purse-proud century may
"sink a middle-aged uncle. He said, looking down
"on the carpet, 'The stockbroker has been here this
"morning, and we are going to dine together at
"Blackwall. He hasn't asked for settlements, and
"we hold to the same creed in politics.' 'There's
"nothing like a Cheap Government,' put in the
"agent with the white hat. I looked down upon this
"sorry pair, who would have been scorched up in
"their chairs had my two eyes been able to wither
"them. 'May all sorts of good luck scamper after
"the Cheap Government and never overtake it!' I
"roared, and so saying bounded into the street, and
"then out of it by the first hansom that passed.
"And here I am eating this tart, and unshakably
"persuaded that, governed cheaply or uncheaply, a
"kingdom given over to stockbrokers must be burned
"up and purified. And I don't believe in the march
"of progress, nor in the flight of time, nor in civil-
"ised negroes, vote by ballot, or the Gulf Stream;
"and everybody I've ever met loved money more
"than wits, and himself more than me; and a fig is
"the most I can say for the lot of them!"

I was much struck by these remarks. We soon
parted, and I walked home pensively; but I don't
think the gooseberries had been cooked enough.

———

No. 2.—The Life-Guardsman.

I WAS walking moodily, as I mostly do, when I became aware of a man who was sitting at an open window in his shirt-sleeves and staring across the road as if I had dropped a shilling which he hoped to pick up. I knew there was no shilling, for I never carry such things, and so, addressing the man with the politeness which has become a second nature with me, I asked him whether he were looking for anything.

Said he: "If you had seen your wife go out of "the front door five minutes ago on the arm of a "Life-Guardsman you would look too until you "bored a hole in the wall."

I felt drawn towards this man from that moment, and stepped upstairs, where he gave me a glass of port and told me the story of his life during two hours and a half by my watch, which keeps good time.

"It is not often," he began, "that boys set up in

"business at ten, but I sold lucifer matches to people
"who wanted them, and to some who didn't, at nine
"and a quarter. The matches were not mine. I wished
"they were. I cannot say whether the course of my
"destiny would have been different if I had sold
"newspapers instead of matches, but I think I might
"have gone on selling newspapers to this day. The
"matches belonged to a man whom they called my
"employer. One morning, after a pensive night, I
"asked him for three times more matches than usual
"and went far away into the country. I have always
"liked the country; the thought of it puts notions
"into my head which I might not otherwise have
"had. Under a shed in an inn-yard, with the sign
"of a blue boar over the door, I saw some faggots
"of firewood carefully stacked as if they had been
"put there for me. I went in and took one and cut
"it into sizes like matches. Then I roamed about
"till I perceived some painters decorating a house,
"and I sat down on a kerbstone eating bread-and-
"cheese and waiting for my opportunity without a
"murmur. By-and-by they went to dinner and left
"their pots of red, blue, and yellow paints in a safe
"place. I walked in and steeped the tips of my
"bits of wood in the paints, after which I set them
"in the sun to dry and presently mixed them with
"my real matches. So it looked as if I had six

"times more than I really had. Appearances are
"often deceitful. Later in the afternoon I was over-
"taken ·by a shower of rain and by a pedlar, who
"spoke kindly to me, and I found in his pocket a
"reel of pink sarsnet. I made up my real matches
"and the painted ones into little bundles, which I
"fastened with the sarsnet. They looked smarter
"than in boxes, and I thought I would sell them
"twice as dear as if they were genuine; which suc-
"ceeded. My experience is that it generally does,
"and I have conducted business on those principles
"ever since. A parson I met one day when I had
"exchanged nearly all my matches for money bought
"two bundles for himself and gave me a shilling.
"He said, 'I like to see a boy earning his own liv-
"ing. Industry, you see, brings its own reward.'
"I took the shilling and answered, 'Yes, it does.'
"'Have you been christened, my boy?' he went
"on. 'No, sir, I hope not,' I said. He looked
"hard and remarked that he supposed I had mis-
"understood him, but added, 'You are a good boy;
"continue as you have begun;' and I promised him
"I would."

The speaker drew his hand thoughtfully across
his brow, and exclaimed, "Finish your port and take
"another glass; it's some I've made myself." I
"answered, "No, thank you," and he proceeded:—

2*

"We were three brothers, who lived on the crest of
"a hill and counted our earnings after dusk. At
"least we loved ourselves like brothers till one of us
"was detected at having more money than the other
"two. They always said it was I, and I have often
"wondered since whether it was. There are facts in
"my career which give me food for reflection now
"and then when I am alone and cast up my ledger.
"I was past twenty at this time, and nobody sang
"out the responses as I did at chapel. I made more
"noise than all the other pews, and people said,
"'You're a religious young man, you won't be long
"in the free seats; Providence'll take care of you.'
"I answered, 'Yes; if I could find a widow with some
"cash I'd marry her and set up a grocer's shop.'
"Our town was piously inclined, and as badly drained
"as most others. There were men in it who had
"new frock-coats and gilt clasps to their prayer-
"books, and when they died it was sorrowful to see
"the masons cover them with slabs of stone and
"send in the bill to their widows. This made the
"widows' tears break out afresh. 'Don't cry so,' I
"said to one of these ladies, who had a black silk
"gown, with crape trimmings, 'the stone cost four
"pounds ten; he can't feel unhappy under it.' 'Oh,
"oh!' she sobbed, 'I shall be miserable all the rest
"of my life. Will you have anything to drink?'

"This widow kept a public with a thirty years'
"ground lease to run, and the fixtures all in good
"repair, and I felt a better man when I looked at
"the barrels of rum, gin, and shrub behind the bar,
"and watched her serve a seven-and-six-penn'orth of
"liquors over the counter in twenty minutes. Said
"I, 'There are loving hearts still left in the world;
"don't put any sugar in my whisky, thank you;' and
"then she continued, drying her eyes with a cotton
"handkerchief and dropping silver into the till, 'I've
"nineteen hundred pounds in the bank, and how I'm
"to spend it all without a husband to help me, good-
"ness only knows.' I was powerfully affected, and
"assured her that the money should never want
"looking after so long as I had a pair of eyes in my
"head. This was in April, whilst it rained, and we
"were married one hot day in June. It was a
"beautiful sight. The sexton felt bad; and the tax-
"gatherer has never been the same man since.
"They were abandoned objects, both of whom I
"pitied, for they had been courting the public house
"which I kept for the widow till she died, which
"was soon; and then I kept it for myself till it was
"burned, not long after I had insured it for a good
"round sum, as I am now grateful to remember. I
"didn't burn with the public, and the insurance
"office was surprised—sadly surprised at it. I wasn't.

"I went in my suit of mourning to receive a cheque
"for £ 5000, and was pained to find a policeman,
"who questioned me about the fire. Said he, 'I've
"my private opinion about you.' Said I, 'You're
"not the first man who's told me that, and you're
"welcome to anything that doesn't cost me money.'
"We talked quietly in this way about the treadmill
"and other personal matters as we strutted along to-
"wards the police-station, side by side, and it struck
"me that he wouldn't have made a good comic singer
"unless he'd been put through a course of training.
"The week after a magistrate said there were no
"proofs, and the insurance office paid me the £ 5000
"with a deep-drawn sigh. They sighed deeper when
"the attorney who was my friend, and smart at law
"tricks, brought a bill of costs and an action for
"slander and false imprisonment. This struck them
"with remorse, and they apologised in a newspaper;
"the policeman apologised too; so did the sexton
"and the tax-gatherer. Everybody was remorseful
"when the attorny took them aside and quoted an
"Act of Parliament out of a book with a calf bind-
"ing; so whilst they were repenting all round, I sold
"the ground lease of my public, and some furniture
"and things which had luckily been out mending
"when the fire broke out; then I drew all my money
"from the bank and came to London with twelve

"thousand pounds in my pocket by an afternoon
"train. I recollect it was a fine murky day, such as
"we all know, and any stranger must have felt
"touched at seeing old men and little boys racing
"about in cabs or on foot to make money in the fog.
"London is a big city, as I cannot but think, and
"there are a mighty number of grocers in it. I my-
"self am now a grocer. I daresay you noticed that
"when coming up through the shop, and if you ever
"eat apricot jam, I've some downstairs, which sells
"well, like my tea, the brown sugar, and the port
"wine in your glass. Profits and attention to busi-
"ness, with here and there giving out tracts for
"heathen missions, have made me rise like a balloon
"over the heads of other folk; for I am an elder of
"my church and a vestryman by this time, and if
"you'll come to chapel next Sunday you'll see me
"hand the plate round. At the board meetings, too,
"and the dinners we have in the workhouse parlour,
"where there's a photograph of Ananias (the last for
"which he ever sat), it's I who make the long speeches;
"and I don't think much of the inspectors who re-
"ported that my weights were short, nor of the
"analysts who declared there were carrots among my
"apricots. Said I, 'When a man's an elder and a
"vestryman, and liable to serve on a jury, there's no
"call to look into his jam-pots, and an extra carrot,

"more or less, doesn't make much difference to those
"who are used to it.' Those are my principles, Sir. I
"never hide them, and I find it sweet to reflect in
"the autumn of a well-spent life that I am a self-
"made man. But now I've married for the second
"time, and my wife has gone walking with the Life-
"Guardsman."

A pregnant silence arose between us at this
meaning climax, and my host beat an abstracted
tattoo on the tray where the port wine was. As for
myself I listened to the voices of customers below
asking for apricot jam, and being supplied with it
by the freckled shop-boy; and my thoughts warmed
to the distant land where apricots first grew before
analysts were ever invented. Nothing but a blue-
bottle broke the taciturnity of our meditations, and
presently he fell into the port wine and was poisoned.
So we sat alone dreaming of the drama that was at
hand, each one absorbed like men with tickets for
an excursion train. And soon there was a rustle on
the staircase, and the misguided wife came in with
honeysuckles in her bonnet, and the Life-Guardsman
behind her. "This is my wife's brother," said my
host, "his name's William; let me introduce you."
The evening shadows were deepening as I faltered,
"Her brother! Why, I imagined——" "No," replied
my host, gloomily, "sometimes I feel mournful sitting

"alone, and I like to have a two hours' talk with a
"stranger. Sit down. Do you like claret better
"than port?"

I felt less drawn towards the man from that
moment, and I have never seen him since.

No. 3.—Mr. Mole.

THE learned judge took his seat on the bench at
eleven o'clock that morning, and began to cry.
Whether it was the heat of the weather or the price
of coals that caused his affliction there is no saying;
but it was noticeable that the prosecutor in this case
had forgotten to wash his face before coming into
court, and that the prisoner stood at the dock with
his hands in his pockets as if he should like to sing
something.

"I'm for the prosecution, my lud," cried Mr. Bawle,
Q.C., springing up.

"And I'm for the defendant," retorted Mr. Wissle,
sitting down.

"Yes," answered his lordship, sadly, "you always
are;" and an usher shouted "Silence!" though
nobody was speaking.

Mr. Bawle rose, with a ream of foolscap in
his hand, and said, "My lud, the case lies in a
"nutshell. The prisoner at the bar, a man of sly

"tongue, named Mole, worked his way into the plain-
"tiff's affections by means of a false character. If
"he had only done that we could have borne it, but
"he sank deep into the heart of the plaintiff's
"daughter, and, what is worse than all, received
"certain salaries for labours which he never per-
"formed, and appropriated other funds for his private
"uses at the public. I shall say nothing of an un-
"pleasant nature, save that the young lady's name
"was Jemima, and that the prisoner took but a single
"hour to persuade her that she was pretty. You shall
"all see for yourselves and judge. When men appeal
"to the law, my lud, it is for redress; when women
"lay bare their inmost feelings and weep for damages,
"it is owing to reasons which nobody need specify."

"I beg to remind you, though," clamoured Mr.
Wissle, with his mouth full of sandwich, "that this
"is a criminal trial, not a civil, and that no damages
"can be obtained even by weeping for them. We
"should live in nice times, forsooth, if——"

"Yes, but we "don't live in nice times," interrupted the judge, making a blot on his note-book,
and licking it up despondently with his tongue,
whilst his tears trickled out afresh by twenties; "I
do not deal in subtleties. "I think you had better
"call your witnesses, brother Bawle—all the witnesses
"you like, and don't mind me."

There was so much pathos in all his lordship said that the five witnesses who then appeared one by one were deeply moved, especially when four of them were caught lying and threatened with Newgate. The first had his arm in a sling; the second thought that two and two made eleven; the next said Devonshire was in Essex; and the two last snivelled through feeling themselves ill-used, which was certainly none of their business. It was proved, however, clearly enough that the man Mole had represented himself as an acute soul, both honest and lively, and had obtained a post and wages in consequence. He turned out to be dull and incapable; that was why he stood in the dock, still keeping his hands in his pockets, and looking as if he should like to sing something if he only dared. His character was produced, written by himself, with plenty of commas and points of admiration where such were needed; and it was generally remarked that the prisoner had not spoken ill of himself in this character, but had dilated feelingly upon his own merits, so that by his own account he seemed to be an earnest person, as Mr. Bawle observed; whereat Mole hummed a tune softly, and looked more than ever as if he should like to sing something.

"Stop a moment, though, I fancy I have read all "this before," exclaimed the judge, examining the document through his tears, and hiccoughing with mournful violence. "Aye, so have I," assented Mr. Wissle, laying his wig over his paper of sandwiches, so that no one should purloin any. At this crisis a policeman, whose tunic was too tight for him, was carried out in hysterics, raving that he had dreamed of the Lord Chief Justice's temper. Another police-man suggested that compensation should be given him from the poor-box, and his proposal was at once complied with. The chief witness of all was then shouted for down a passage, and being intro-duced swore that her name was Jemima. She was told to lift up her veil and tell the truth, which she did by pulling out her handkerchief and sneezing wildly.

"Many's the time that I've been deceived be-
"fore," she sobbed, "but never so cruelly as by
"Mr. Mole. He stuck to facts at first, and said
"I was young and lovely, sweet and sensible,
"pious and kind to a fault; all which being true
"we kept company together down by the water-
"side, and I fried fish for his tea and stewed him
"plums in sugar. Then I found that by watching
"his behaviour it was the plums, and not me, that
"he loved; for he scalded me with hot water and led
"me into puddles, saying it was' all for my health,
"and that he knew better than I what was good for

"me. When I heard him say that, I screamed at him
"at day and night till he vowed he should like to
"go if anyone would take his place—which nobody
"would, not even curly Ben, whom I winked at, but
"who said he'd tried me before and had had enough
"of me. Then Mole growing rampageous and scald-
"ing me again and again, not to mention fresh
"puddles at every step, so that the mud lay thick
"on my clothes, and the other girls laughed at me
"for a fright—then I said to myself, 'Is this the
"Mole that we read of in the character, with all his
"good qualities clustering thick as grapes?' and I
"decided no, that it couldn't be the same Mole, or
"else that he had hoaxed us by writing his own
"character for himself out neat with a new steel pen
"and quotations from the Bible. Which so it was,
"as we discovered by inquiry; and that's why he
"stands yonder trying to look holy and cool, as if
"butter wouldn't melt in his mouth. But he's a bad
"'un."

Nothing could paint the conviction which this
harangue carried home even to the breast of the
most hardened listener; though the prisoner seemed
cogitating what manner of song he should sing as
soon as he recovered his liberty. The judge's moans
were heard through the open windows as far as St.
Sepulchre's, and the trial proceeded on its deep,

silent way. Messrs. Bawle and Wissle made speeches till luncheon, then wordily went at it again till the day was far spent and the evening at hand; whereupon the judge summed up his impressions on a slate, being too overcome to speak, and the prisoner hummed the first bars of "Would you love me then "as now" in a gentle voice, whilst the jury retired to consider their verdict. At sunset they were still considering, at midnight half of them had escaped over the roofs, at 2.30 a.m. the last juryman was descried eating cake with the judge at an early coffee-stall, and the rumour was spread in the dark that the prisoner had unaccountably vanished, leaving in his cell a song entitled "They all do it" and a statement in pencil to the effect that he would advise no one who could help it to face the verdict of a jury.

No. 4.—The Yellow Dog.

HE could not have spoken more pathetically if he had been on the road to be hanged; and I followed his directions, judging that a man who talked so wisely could not but tell the truth. He said I must turn to the right, then to the left, and walk straight on for a few hours or so till I reached the place I wanted—that is the Tell-Tale Torrent, where sat the Girl with the Mocking Eyes.

I started and arrived, and saw the water fall in foaming cascades over the rocks, dashing up a spray of diamonds and wetting to the skin a small boy who was sitting on his heels and pelting frogs out of a hamper-full of pebbles which he kept near him for the purpose. But he did not seem to mind being wet, and the Girl with the Mocking Eyes sat opposite him on the other bank, laughing to see the frogs take headers to avoid the pebbles, and dabbling her bare feet in the stream as it hurried frothing by her.

Her golden hair was as fine as spun glass, she had a blue skirt and a scarlet bodice, with a chemisette of lawn, and her sleeves fell but two inches below her shoulders. Beside her was a hamper like the boy's, but the lid was down, closed securely with a silver chain and padlock, and corded with pink ribbons; also, for greater safety's sake, she rested one of her elbows on the lid as if it were a pillow and the velvet moss on which she lay a sofa.

She started up on catching sight of me, and the boy, without ceasing to pelt his frogs, shouted as a welcome,

"You're another!"

"What do you mean by another?" I inquired, resting on my stick and feeling for my flask, for the ascent up the rocks had been long and steep.

"Oh! I know all about it," replied the boy; "they come here by dozens, and it's my business to "fish them out of the water when she pitches them "in. Look, here's a hook and a rope, so I shan't "let you drown."

"I don't want to drown, my boy."

"No, you needn't unless you're bent upon it; but "you know her conditions?" I confessed I was aware of no conditions, seeing that I had breakfasted early and walked seven hours along a road with no trees to it and much out of repair. He took up the biggest pebble he could find and flung it with such precision into the torrent that it struck a speckled frog on the nape of the neck just where his shirt-collar ought to have been, caused him to spin round legs uppermost, and vanish for evermore from human gaze. "You are a cruel boy," I remarked; but his only acknowledgment was to draw forth a pocket-book, where he entered a score with his thumb-nail and muttered, "That makes the "fifteenth frog; and now listen." He stood up, brushing his knees with his hands, and with a voice that had not a quaver in it recited the conditions:

"You may attempt three times to kiss her, and "if you succeed she will give you a present out of "her hamper such as no man or woman alive save "she could give you. But if you fail you will be "her servant for six weeks and will have to kneel "on the bank beside me and pelt frogs, or she will "send you into the square field a mile off to look "after newts and stag-beetles."

"Yes, but if I don't make any attempt to kiss "her?"

"Ah, it's too late now!" replied the boy; "you've "come here and must do like the rest." The Girl laughed from the other bank, and there was a mocking devil in that laugh. She had broken off a long

willow switch and whistled it before her face as if
to warn me of what was in store. "What's your
"name, my pretty child?" I cried politely; but she
said, "Never mind my name," and only laughed
the louder, which was like adding, "Kiss me if you
"dare!"

Now I am not vainer than other men, but have
always thought that no girl could look upon my features without loving me; so I laid down my stick,
put my knapsack beside it, and set my felt hat at
the top of both to prevent the wind blowing them
away. I reflected later that I ought to have put the
hat undermost, but first thoughts are never so good
as second, in addition to which I was concerned as
to how I might cross the stream, which was deep,
and made a violent noise.

I crossed it by means of four rocks which the
boy showed me at a turning fifty yards down, and
being on the same side as the Girl I advanced towards her, smiling, yet not liking the look of that
switch. She retreated, dancing and singing; I followed, and it was not long before we stood together
on a jutting ledge of rock overhanging the most
rapid part of the stream—in fact, just below the
cascade.

She ceased receding then, and it occurred to me
that after all she might be only coquetting. But

3*

just as this conclusion had shaped itself in my mind she dealt me with the switch and right across the face the most tingling cut I had ever heard of, and without leaving me time to recover, stepped forward, cuffed me with all her laughing might on the left ear, and sent me headlong among the frogs into ten fathoms of water, with the cataract roaring above like a whole orchestra of devils.

"Never say die," sang out the boy and planting his harpoon into a section of my garments below the waist he dragged me backwards to the bank, whereon I scrambled half-drowned, bruised, and feeling as if my left ear had swollen to twice the size of my head. Meantime the wind had blown my hat away into a swamp, but I didn't care, for I foamed with chagrin and humiliation; and let me add at once that the Girl with the Mocking Eyes cuffed me into the water a second time, and that the boy stuck his harpoon into me as before and landed me with considerable skill, as if he were used to the work.

The third time I mused bitterly upon my lot—should I be forced to pelt frogs for six weeks or attend to the stag-beetles, and I proceeded cautiously, with a sort of musical accompaniment from my boots, which sang *queak*, *queak*, as though to make sport of me. It was a pensive walk up those fifty yards of bank, for both my ears were now swollen, and if I could have looked into a glass I was sure I should have seen my face ornamented with two pink weals, like a St. Andrew's cross. She awaited my coming with a firm foot, her eyes darting mirthful sparks, and the switch whistling with a keener sound than ever.

"You are very pretty," I observed, pausing at a respectful distance; "but I wish you would throw "that switch down and put your hands behind "you."

"I daresay," she rejoined, and at the same time laughed so derisively that I ejaculated, "I'll give up "the attempt, for it's no use. I'll pelt the frogs and "attend to the stag-beetles, only tell me why you "are so cruel."

She tripped down joyously from her ledge of rock, cast away the switch, and exclaimed, "Now "you are my servant;" but my renunciation was all a stratagem, and seeing her unarmed I darted forward, caught her round the waist, and in despite of scratches and blows, of which she was not chary, kissed her thrice on the lips. "That's not fair," she cried, disentangling herself wildly, and giving me one more avenging slap, smarter than any of the previous ones; but the boy on the opposite side yelped, "Yes, it's quite fair, it's in the conditions,"

and he danced on his head for pure glee, for it
turned out he was a good boy, with a soul above
his trade.

The Girl stood quivering a moment and glaring
at me; but at length she laughed and gave a shrug,
blushing, "Well, I ought to have been prepared for
"the deceit of men; but I shall know better another
"time.   Come along, you have won a present, only
"mind it shall be what present I please;" saying
which she ran to the hamper, unlocked it with a
key that hung like a locket round her neck, and
drew out a yellow puppy wrapped in a number of
the *Spectator*.

"I wrap him in the *Spectator*," she exclaimed,
"because it keeps him asleep.   And now, hark! this
"dog will howl whenever he hears a lie told, or sees
"any book or writing that contains untruths or hypo-
"crisy.   He is yours, and you need never be de-
"ceived again so long as he is in your company.
"But recollect if ever you want to get rid of him
"you must come back and take this key from my
"neck, which isn't so easy, for you shall not deceive
"me twice."

Uttering which remark she laughed mockingly,
according to her wont, whilst I, considering my property, suggested that he was very small.   "Oh, but
"I'll make him bigger," said she, and placing him

on her lap she pulled at his tail, ears, and legs, all of which lengthened immediately, like telescopes, so that the dog was soon of a poodle's size, and large enough according to my fancy. This done she wished me an ironical good-bye, and inquired archly whether the switch had hurt me. Not wishing to be uncivil I said "No," whereat my yellow dog inaugurated his duties with a prolonged howl, which much amused the Girl, as also the boy, and served to remind me of the valuable gift that had been bestowed on me. I said nothing more, but bowed and hurried off, my dog declining to go into the marsh and fish out my hat as I had hoped he would do. He was, in truth, a proud and sage dog, above menial service.

Yes, above menial service—above everything but truth-telling; and now sympathise with me for the possession of an animal which has not left me an hour's quiet since I have been his master. He howled when the inn-keeper brought me my bill, he howled when the cabman stated his fare at the station, and he howled longer and more weirdly on the platform opposite the notice which professed to say when the trains started. He has howled when I met friends and said I was glad to see them; he has howled still louder when the friends declared they were glad to see me. On account of his noise

I have been obliged to give up reading the *Times*, and at the mere sight of the *Daily Telegraph* the whole street is filled with his wailings. Depressed by his conduct I went out one night and tried to lose him, but he was found howling outside a mansion in Carlton House Terrace, and the policeman who brought him home assured me he had interrupted a political conference of great pith and moment. Mr. Gladstone, who was my friend, will have nothing to say to me since he was bayed at by my yellow dog, and several other eminent politicians have voted him a cordial nuisance. Sir E. Henderson warned me amicably that I must not take the dog up Whitehall, nor on the Thames whilst Parliament was sitting, nor near Westminster Hall at any time, and still less near the Court of Chancery. The Attorney-General, hearing of the brute, came and wished to retain him in some law suits, but the dog howled so many times and so lugubriously in the course of his first day in court, that the scheme was abandoned there and then. Not wishing to be actioned for libel, I can mention neither the books, nor the speeches, nor the sermons at sight or sound of which this precious dog of mine has made his dismal voice heard; but I may state that in hopes of getting fairly rid of him I sent him as a present not long ago to a statesman whose earnestness, singleness of purpose, and deep love of truth have been a source of untold blessings to these islands. I trusted the yellow dog might be for ever silenced in his society; but alas, it was but yesterday the parcels-delivery brought me back my too candid cur with a note on official paper stating that he had howled continuously from sunrise to bed-time.

What shall I do with this beast? Who wants a truth-telling dog—a genuine bargain for an upright and pious people? He can be had cheap—or even as a gift by any respectable family of Britons who will undertake to keep him for a twelvemonth.

No. 5.—The Moss Rose.

I COULD easily tell you the name of the policeman if I had not forgotten it, but what I know is
this—that after hearing the pitiful story of the little
girl with the moss rose he dealt himself three severe
blows on the head with his truncheon, being determined to live no longer in a world where such
injustice existed. I could not but approve his conduct on this occasion, though not liking the sight of
blood I followed the little girl into the street, and
dismissed all that concerned the policeman from my
memory. The little girl had bare feet and a draggled
gown, but her eyes were of a hazel-like dark cairn-
gorm, and she held the moss-rose to her lips with
both hands as if the morning breezes wished to take
it from her.

"That is a sweet-smelling flower, my pretty
"child," I exclaimed, and asked her if she would sell
it me, volunteering to give her whatever price she
desired within reason that is within twopence or

so. But she placed her back against the railings of a house which had a bird-stuffer's name on the door, and shook her head as she answered, "It is the "sweetest rose that ever grew in the sunlight, and "nobody knows its worth nor what it can do; but I "will never sell it or give it away;" saying which she gently stroked the flower as if it were a pet she loved.

"Never?" I echoed, regretfully, and perhaps I may have sighed, for she raised her eyes and examined me curiously a moment, evidently wondering whether I were a man to be trusted.

"Perhaps," added she, in a relenting voice, "per-"haps I may drop it on the ground, and then you "may pick it up, but you must promise to be always "kind to the mice and never to hurt them. They "were good to me one night and made me laugh "when no one else cared whether I was alive or "dead. It was a night when it froze, and I slept on "a doorstep till a policeman like the one you saw "came and told me to move on." She ceased speaking, and I thought she must have gone into the bird-stuffer's, for she had vanished unaccountably, and was not to be seen on the pavement or down the area; besides which all the stuffed birds in the window appeared to be making sport of me. However, the moss-rose lay on the ground, so I picked it up and stuck it in my button-hole.

There lived with me in my chambers at that time a mouse; but I was not on speaking terms with him. He ate the best chapters out of my books, and I had warned him that a persistence in these ways must lead to my borrowing a cat, though I fancied such an addition to our circle even less than he did. So far from paying heed to my remonstrances he took to himself a wife, whereat, judging by the precedents in such cases that there would soon be an increase, not of one, but of six or eight to our joint establishment, I had resolved that the mouse must turn over a new leaf or die. But when I put the little girl's moss-rose into my coat it seemed to me as if I bound myself by treaty to let the mouse be—nay, to set a piece of Stilton every evening within his reach, so that he might dine in peace, he and his nearest relatives, if he had any.

I cannot understand the various other new springs of thought which the contact of this rose opened up; but I felt I was not the same man as before. The rose's perfume filled the air and charmed me; it also charmed others. I walked along smiling and being smiled at, gathering pleasant impressions where on other days I had seen nothing in particular to admire, and reflecting at every step how odd it was that the world had never seemed to me gay and habitable as then. When I reached my chambers the mouse came out upon the carpet as if he were willing to forgive and forget, and he danced before me into a corner that I might witness the event he had long been awaiting with a father's anxiety. The sight was not unimpressive, for the mouse flourished his tail over the bridal retreat to chase intruding flies away; and he conveyed to me, with simple dignity enough, that mother and children were doing well in one of my dress boots.

I mused a moment, and said, as I looked at him and he at me, "Can you tell, fortunate mouse, what "is the meaning of this sudden dilation of heart and "soul that possesses me at this moment? You are "welcome to my boots and my books—which you "never were till now—and I will open the provision "cupboard for you this very evening; but give me "an explanation of this phenomenon in as lucid a "manner as you can, and when you get into the "cupboard beware of the brandy and Chili pickles, "which would disagree with you." The mouse intimated by a gesture that he never refused an answer to a civil question, and jumping over the boot-jack he climbed on to my desk and thence on to a

Webster's Dictionary lying open there, and scored a mark with his teeth at the word "ILLUSION."

But this was all I could extract from him, for he withdrew in a hurry to busy himself about his domestic concerns, and I was fain to go out into the streets and inquire of every connoisseur I met why this rose of mine so far outshone all other roses in perfume and colour. I questioned flower-girls at street corners and florists in Covent Garden, I called at nursery-gardeners' and scientific horticulturists', and from one and all I got the same reply:—"That "bud of yours is the famous Illusion-Rose, and we "advise you never to part with it."

I had no wish to part with it, but the counsel of all these people set me brooding, I remembered what the little bare-footed girl had said about nobody's knowing the rose's value nor what it could do, and by slow reflection I came gradually to guess that I held a rose every leaf of which represented an illusion—that is, a certain sum of confidence and hope.

Shall I tell you now how one by one these pretty rose-leaves were swept away as I roamed about the world, smiling less and less, but carrying the flower ever with me? I think it was an hotel waiter who brushed off the first leaf as I was asking him for a bottle of sound claret. He brought the wine, but the pink leaf lay crumbled near my glass's stem, and I knew that I was drinking logwood. A states-man broke off the second, button-holing me familiarly and explaining to me his policy, which I might have thought a fine one had I retained my rose-leaf. Picture-dealers, actresses who looked houris on the stage and were painted old women off it, newspaper writers who spoke stirringly in print and laughed at themselves and their readers when standing with chums near a club fire, canters and pretenders of all degrees and professions, tore off my leaves—some mockingly, some gravely, but all marvelling to see me wince as they watched the poor honest little things fluttering to the ground. I soon became rated, as was natural, for a curious fellow, over-sensitive and non-appreciating. I lost many friends and gained none.

Meantime my leaves continued to fall, and now I have but a single one remaining, though so long a time has elapsed since the flower came into my possession that I humbly venture to hope this one relic of it may bide with me to the end. It is as fresh and sweet-smelling as on the day it first glad-dened me with its fellows, and possibly each of the other leaves as they died may have bequeathed to it some of their scent and brilliancy to make it compensate me for having lost them all. My mouse is long dead, and so are his children and grand-children; but an hour ago I questioned a young mouse who I suspect is descended from the old one and bade him tell me what final illusion is represented by my surviving leaf. With a courtesy which seemed bred of family tradition he scrambled as his ancestor had done on to the dictionary and nibbled a little hole opposite the word "LOVE."

No. 6.—Proverbial Philosophy.

MORE puzzling than all was the conduct of the Town Clerk, who had mislaid the corporation-seal in the coal-scuttle, and who, when he sat down to table put the largest pat of butter into his waistcoat-pocket and said, "Don't mention it." I do mention it, because one or two supposed at the time that he must have intended to pocket something else; but the impulses of his mind were devious, and he had lost all his front teeth from thinking about the public weal. I can only say for my part that I found in him a man of subtle wit and excellent sense, and that he was most obliging in giving me directions which I could not quite understand. But he added that I should certainly obtain all the particulars I wanted by calling on the "Lady who talked Greek."

My business was not about Greek, but about getting my rooms new papered, only the paper I required was one that should convey to me sound moral maxims whilst I dressed of a morning and

took tea in the evening. My friends had a great
opinion of proverbs; and there can be no doubt that
many men might be cautioned against the practice
of early-rising by remembering the fate of the too
early worm, while certain others might possibly be
dissuaded from staying at home by thinking over
that stone which stuck fast in one place and gathered
a good deal of moss which could have been of no
manner of use to it.   A paper stamped with several
hundreds of proverbs like these would have met my
case, and made me, by degrees, I hoped, as wise as
the son who knew his own father.

   So I knocked at the door of the Lady who
talked Greek, and was surprised to notice that the
house had no resemblance to a paper-hanger's,
though there was in truth a proverbial expression
about the face of the butler who answered my summons, for I presently learned that he had been handsome once and had ceased to be so now, thus veri-
fying the adage that "A thing of beauty is a joy for
ever."   He showed me into a drawing-room which
others might have deemed well-furnished, but I reserved my impressions knowing that appearances are
deceitful; and in a few minutes' time there tripped
in a girl of twenty, dressed in a light blue silk, with
a white rose in her girdle, who said: "I presume
"you've called to see mamma, but I'm sorry to say

"she sprained her wrist this morning in lifting a
"volume of Lord Houghton's poems off the bookshelf,
"for it was a very heavy volume."

I smiled, and answered gallantly: "'Tis sweet to
"suffer for those we love. If your mamma loves
"Houghton's poems she must derive unusual bliss
"from the pain in her wrist; besides which it's an ill
"wind that blows nobody good, and if your mamma
"were not happily unwell, I should not enjoy the
"good fortune of seeing you, who are doubtless no-
"thing but a heap of dust like us all, but never-
"theless very pretty dust."

"How odd you are!" she replied, staring; "but
"I have heard about you from the Town Clerk, who
"comes now and then to take tea with us, and who
"promised to bring you some night—you and your
"album of sea-weeds."

"I never had an album of sea-weeds," was my
mournful rejoinder; "and all I want is about a hun-
"dred square yards of wall-paper with instructive
"axioms on it: '*Anger is the politeness of kings;*'
"'*Punctuality is a brief madness;*' and so forth."

"Well, I never!" she ejaculated, clasping her
hands; "that Town Clerk has been committing an-
"other of his mistakes. Why last week he sent us
"the butterman, and we mistook him for Mr. Martin

"Tupper. After giving him a long dinner mamma "asked him to write something in her autograph "book, and he wrote, 'Thankful for past favours and "anxious for a continuance of the same.' I declare "it's too bad, and I think the Town Clerk is be-"coming crazy. Everybody says so."

"Never trust rumour," I interposed, thoughtfully; "the devil is not so black as he is painted."

"What do you know about it?" inquired the young girl in blue, with a laugh; "you'ye never seen "him nor anyone else either."

Now this was a poser, and set me reflecting. After all, no one to my certain knowledge *has* ever seen the devil, yet I have frequently been told that I must give him his due—which would seem to imply a notion of his oft-recurring presence like that of the tax-gatherer. I took a seat on a sofa near the fireplace, and requesting the girl in blue to do the same buried my head in my hands for a while and pondered silently over the question of proverbial paper as against plain paper. Glancing through my fingers now and then as I thus mused it struck me that my interlocutrix looked comelier every moment, and I fell to regretting somehow that she had a mother who talked Greek. She on her side considered me with apparent interest, and it was inevitable that I should meditate how well-matched a pair we might make.

Meanwhile the fire burned brightly, the coal sparks danced upwards, and before long a purse flew with a loud bang out of the grate and settled on the hearth-rug. This gave the girl an opportunity of screaming sweetly and me the occasion of displaying my presence of mind and love of order by restoring the coal with the tongs to its proper place. The thing was romantically done on both sides, and if it be true that it needs but a spark to light a flame it was assuredly that timely coal which lit up the eloquence that consumed me for the next quarter of an hour. I announced that after giving the matter my best thoughts I was resolved to paper my rooms with sheets of Mr. Tupper's "Proverbial Philosophy," and that nothing should deter me from this course short of possessing a wife whose wisdom would stand me in lieu of Mr. Tupper's, and who should furthermore look well in a sky-blue dress. The young lady blushed and glanced down at the carpet, and so did I. But there was such an ominous method in my vow that she presently faltered,

"I wouldn't do that if I were you. Can't you "live singly without proverbs?"

"Two heads are better than one," was my emphatic response; "and Mr. Tupper's head and mine "will steer me more safely through the rocks of life "than would mine alone. You surely believe in "utterers of wise saws?"

She hesitated a moment, then made a dissentient gesture with her hand, and turning pink again said: "No, I do not; for if you have been to school you "will remember these lines, which cover "all your philosophers with just the cap that fits "them:—

Οὐκ ἔργον ἐστίν εὖ λέγειν, ἀλλ' εὖ ποιεῖν
Πολλοὶ γὰρ εὐλέγοντες οὐκ ἔχουσι νοῦν. *

A pregnant silence ensued, during which hat and umbrella found their way on to the floor and remained there. I gazed at the girl first sternly, then with incipient purpose of resentment, and at last remarked gravely: "It's you then who talk "Greek, and not your mother?" To which she coolly replied: "Mamma talks Greek, and we are going to "learn Afghanese together next winter, *if I've nothing "better to do!*"

What more shall I add? I had entered the house

---

* For those who have mislaid their lexicons: "It is not hard to spout, but it is hard to act well; for many men of fluent speech have little brains."

in the morning a free man, with a proverb on my
lips; I left it late in the afternoon muttering a new
proverb well worth laying to heart: "Man proposes
"and—Woman seldom refuses."

No. 7.—The Glass Eye.

No one could see clearer through difficulties than the Man with the Glass Eye, and his friends never had him to dinner without feeling that they and their belongings sat under his thoughtful scrutiny. If you showed him a bill for £5 and asked him how to pay it, he seldom reflected long before answering, "Don't pay it;" and if times were bad, he was bad with them, not caring to shame them by an affectation of superior virtue. One, thinking to puzzle him, asked him how to lead a red-headed boy up the paths of virtue; but he replied, "Travel that way "yourself, and perhaps the young un 'll follow you." Now this querist, being a milkman whose religion consisted more in roaring "Hallelujah!" than in keeping chalk out of his pails, never again sought advice from the Man with the Glass Eye.

Three of us, however, having sown our wild oats and found the crop yield well, had determined on marriage, less because we liked the idea than because man was not intended to live alone, except when he likes quiet. We called on the Man with the Glass Eye and paid him each a guinea, which he locked in a drawer, then took his stand on the hearth-rug, with his coat-tails under his arms, and thus spoke:—

"You are going to be married and have come "to me for approval. I never approve of such things, "and am not going to derogate from a time-honoured "habit in order to please you. Neither, if you anti-"cipate happiness, shall I encourage any such ground-"less belief, having now in my pocket a letter from "a haberdasher who married last year and wished "himself well out of it last week. That haberdasher "is one of many. The tin boxes on those shelves "are full of letters from men who wished themselves "well out of it; some have gone mad, others shed "tears till there was no keeping one's clothes dry in "their company, a few were distrained on by the "grocer and allowed all the nap on their hats to "moult away for grief. Those examples will not "deter you, for they never do; but I will give each "of you a glass eye like mine, and you shall judge "for yourselves whether the bargains you are going "to make will be worth the cost of a licence, fees "to a vicar, and other expenses both weighty and "ridiculous."

So saying this man had recourse to his left coat-tail and drew forth three purple morocco cases, such as jewellers use to enclose rings. He handed one to each of us, bidding us observe that it contained a light shell of opaque glass, concave in shape, and illustrated with the pupil of an eye well limned; then he proceeded:—

"What is beauty? A thing of mind, not of mat-"ter. If you knew that a girl were trying to put "arsenic into your soup, should you agree that her "features were sweet and womanly? No; then beauty "is a delusion of the eyesight—an outward lure which "would vanish if you could behold the moral ugli-"ness within. Those glass eyes will give you that "power of inner-sight. You there" (turning to me) "ought to have no need of such help, for 'you were "presented with a yellow dog who howled bravely "when he heard an untruth; but you parted from "him because you and your talkative friends found "him too candid, and that was a pity, for if you had "kept him till now you might have read him some "of your betrothed's love-letters and gathered his "opinions on them. However, attend to these glass "eyes, for they will show you men and women "exactly as they would be if each of their vices or "foibles were represented by some bodily blemish. "Falsehood will be figured by a wide and dribbling

"mouth; greed and sensuality by monstrous lips;
"curiosity and cunning by an overgrown nose and
"blear eyes; laziness by a club foot; rapacity by
"talon-claws; and to sum up, every vile thought will
"have left its stigma in a wrinkle or a mole, whilst
"all the base and wicked acts will have accumulated
"in humps of more or less bigness between the
"shoulders. But to make everything plainer here is
"a printed key." And this time our adviser extracted
from his right coat-tail three tracts with black covers
thus intituled: "*Catalogue of Human Deformities,*
"*carefully revised and enlarged by the Man with the*
"*Glass Eye.*" "There's one apiece for you," he
added, civilly. "And now please remember that
"although I have lent glass eyes to hundreds of men
"before you the boon has never rendered practical
"service to any of them."

"And why not?" inquired one of us three who
was bolder than the other two.

"Because I claim no power to diminish the num-
"ber of simpletons," responded the Man with the
Glass Eye, laughing grimly. "I can unmask Vice,
"but I cannot make you hate her; in that attempt
"finer Stoics than I have failed before me, and will
"continue to fail so long as this queer earth is peo-
"pled as it is. Are there less drunkards because
"drink is known to be disgusting and poisonous?

"Do men plunge less into crime, women into sin,
"and humanity generally into the silly pits of mean-
"ness, falsehood, and sordid villanies because liars,
"wantons, and criminals are branded with ignominy
"and lead shameful lives? Not a bit of it. Then
"go your ways: wilful blindness is an ailment that
"no magic can cure."

"Excuse me," I interrupted, with a presence of
mind to which I am now and then subject; "excuse
"me, but if my glass eye showed me a girl to be
"hump-backed, blear-eyed, wide-mouthed, and claw-
"fingered, I hope you do me the justice to suppose
"that I should abstain from marrying her."

"Tut, tut!" he replied, shrugging his shoulders
so high that I expected he would knock his ears off.
"Peace, man! look at those tin boxes—but I have
"no time to waste in prating. The way to use those
"glass optics is to slip them under the left eyelid;
"when you have seen enough of the world in its
"true colours, then cover the glass eye with your
"hand or take it out altogether. Now go along and
"enjoy yourselves."

We went along as requested, but enjoying ourselves was another matter. For myself I put on my
glass eye going down the staircase, and I was no
sooner through the front door than I clutched hold
of the area railings, staggering in terror at the sight

which offered itself to my view. The thoroughfare
was a populous one, but instead of being crowded
with ordinary men and women it was filled with
throngs of monsters such as I should have thought
not the nethermost abyss itself could have vomited.
Writhing hunchbacks with the leer of fiends, mis-
shapen cripples with lolling tongues, women whose
horrible jaws would have swallowed big crabs alive,
gibbering idiots, sluts, shrivelled hags atwist and
cramped with wickedness—such were the beings who
elbowed one another and made the prospect hideous
as far as the eye could reach. Animals alone—those
whom we call dumb brutes—had escaped the general
deformity; and, seeing horses prance in their grace-
ful vigour, dogs trot with their honest tails on the
wag, shapely birds carol in the pride and glee of
innocence, I thought of man's power over the other
orders of creation and sighed with shame and pity
at it.

Then I turned and beheld that my two companions had become transfigured; and, worse than
all, that I too was changed in their eyes, for one of
them recoiled from my touch and cried as if I had
bitten him, "Why, what's the matter with your
"ears?"

"Ah, my ears!" I roared, indignantly; "I like
"your talking about my ears when your nose has

"swelled to the size of a pig's snout, proving you
"to have been always a poking, prying fellow at
"bottom."

"Hark to him! he speaks of my snout," screamed
my whilom friend in a voice that cracked right
through the middle from fury; "why, look at your
"own! it's a trunk—a proboscis!" And the other
friend, whose mouth would have gone right round
his head if it had not been stopped by his shirt-
collar, displayed a set of tusks notched like domi-
noes, and yelped, "It's a trunk—a proboscis!"

We parted on hot terms, heaping malisons on
one another, and I rushed down the street, scaring
cripples, hunchbacks, and the whole misbegotten crew
by the withering glances I shot at them. A cabman
touched his hat to me, but his countenance was
pitted like a sieve from filching thoughts, and his
forefinger was like a vulture's claw; another would
have beguiled me into an omnibus, but the rogue's
back was bent under a hump as large as a pedlar's
pack, and he pocketed a half-sovereign which he
had received in mistake for a sixpence even as he
hailed me. At a corner I ran into the arms of a
policeman whose lips were swollen with perjuries,
and not desiring to be charged on the oath of himself and a dozen more with being drunk and fractious, I sped into a shop and saw a grocer weigh

out a pound of adulterated mustard, a fine mole blossoming on his nose's tip as he declared this article to be genuine.

Such were the results of my first few minutes' experience; but how describe the afternoon I spent exploring all the nooks of London life to see if perchance I might find one single man who walked straight, had no wrinkles, and sported features of fair proportions? I met no such paragon, nor anything resembling it, save an idiot whose ears grew over the top of his head and curled flat on it like wet rags. This one had a smooth face, for he thought no evil, having no wits to think with; but he was generally looked upon as a disgrace to his family, and his parents spoke of him with humiliation.

Elsewhere I perceived men with bulging knees huge as pumpkins, and referring to my catalogue I knew them to be slippery statesmen who had climbed to power by truckling and kneeling to mobs' bluster. Then again crooked fellows with gnarled fingers eaten up by warts, and these were writers who sold their pens to the highest bidder and argued truth away six times a-week at five or two guineas the column. Other great censors and leaders of men I saw hobbling along with their sins oozing from them like gum and snails off a pear tree; but what troubled me more than all was to observe the women.

Again and again I covered the glass eye with my hand to see whether the ghastly apparitions that flashed by me in broughams and barouches were indeed the radiant women I was wont to bow to in society, and every time I did this the familiar smiles, soft eyes, and modest faces reappeared. But when I withdrew my hand it was as if a blight had fallen: features wrinkled up like walnut shells, eyes sank abashed into their orbits and glowered there like dull coals, and the tell-tale humps rose towering between the shoulders. Then I, a man in love, noting these things and remembering that I had borrowed my glass eye in order to take a moral survey of the maiden I was about to espouse for better or for worse, I, that man in love, caught fright. For was it worth while to tear up the one illusion that was left me when by simply dropping my glass eye down an area I might retain my belief in the exceptional moral beauty of at least one woman?

There was an area close to me—a fashionable milliner's area down which a young potman with a face like a caricature had just slunk to exchange beer and kisses with a housemaid devilish to look upon. Over the spikes of the area I was gazing in doubtful mood, when a brougham clattered up, and

I heard a well-known tiny voice exclaim, "Dear me! "is that you?" . . .

The glass eye did not go down the area. It flashed with the intentness of a policeman's lantern full on the brougham, and—there she sat, naïve and wondering, but winsome as ever, with her little lips apart, and her features clear as Truth's—spotless, sinless, blameless. If I could have thought that my glass eye was playing me false, the fear would not have lasted long, for beside my future wife sat my future mother-in-law, who looked—but let us tread lightly over that matter. It was enough for me that there existed but one woman on earth in whom my magic eye could discover no blemish, and that one was the woman whom I had most interest in knowing to be perfection.

And now a moral. I put back the glass eye into my pocket, but learning soon that my two friends had perceived that their respective brides were also faultless, I hurried to see whether this thing were true or not, and found, as I had well anticipated, that the thing was not true. I held my peace however, for seeing these deluded friends lovingly encircle the waists of a pair of ladies who, to the keen vision of my glass eye, seemed directly descended from the Eumenides and Harpies, a new light broke upon me. I recalled the caution of the

Man with the Glass Eye, I thought of the rows of tin boxes, of the haberdasher's letter, of the man whose hat moulted for grief, and I bowed my head to this very old adage, that "We are all of us blind "to the faults of those we love." Now I have dispossessed myself of my glass eye. I sent it some time back to the Prime Minister, who promised me to use it in selecting candidates for posts of emolument; and I may add, without violating secrecy, that it has already been of great service to him and to the public at large. All Government functionaries are nowadays irreproachable.

No. 8.—The Ten Clocks.

WE know that Adam died at the age of nine
hundred and thirty from grief at being unable to
attain his thousandth year. Many men are thus
baulked in the pursuit of a laudable object to which
they have devoted the energies of a life-time, and I
have always pitied them. The man who sought to
clothe himself in his own purity, the other one who
tried sliding down hill as a cure for the toothache,
and the more benighted person who attempted to
make his wife hear reason, are all examples of a
fruitless ambition. But the most conspicuous case
which has ever come to my knowledge is that of
the man who thirsted after the Spirit of Concord,
and who meant well, though nothing ever came of
his meaning.

This man thought we should be happier if we
all watched the march of events from the same
point of view. He was a subscriber to the ten
newspapers which appear daily in London, and it

5*

grieved him to perceive that in each newspaper there was a different point of view, which sometimes made ten points of view to one event and created confusion. Yet, as he justly argued, there could be but one true point of view, and, being a man who took much for granted, he assumed that if he could explain to the ten London editors that an event must, like a colour, be black, white, or red, but could not be red, black, white, and indigo all together, these editors would thank him for this information and act upon it.

He was not wholly mistaken, for the editors said they would thank him to walk out, which he did forthwith, though he marvelled somewhat and was not deterred from his valuable idea. Much the contrary, for seeing it was near midnight when he was kicked—I mean shown—out of the last newspaper office, he made for Printing House Square, and took a few turns round it on one leg to collect his impressions. This done he leaned against a lamp-post and twelve o'clock chiming rhythmically at that moment from a neighbouring steeple, a shadowy figure emerged from the *Times* office, stalked swiftly into the little square and confronting the man against the lamp-post, said: "Who are you, "and what do you want?"

"I am searching for the Spirit of Concord," an-

swered the man against the lamp-post, surveying
the Shadow intently, but nothing daunted, and he
added: "If you can give me that Spirit I shall be
"pleased."

"Ah! but I can't," replied the Shadow mournfully, "for they never kept it on sale in my time;
"we were content with gin and rum."

"Nobody ever spoke to you of gin or rum,"
protested the man against the lamp-post, licking his
lips, and he noticed that the Shadow had a devil-
may-care look, but wore neat shoe-strings like Sir
William Harcourt's.

"Nothing can be rummer than the Spirit of
"Concord," remarked the Shadow, chuckling dryly
as if his jaws wanted oiling. "Concord kept the
"cat and dog at peace, but I doubt whether it made
"them happier. Anyhow I like your idea of bring-
"ing all newspapers to take but one view of facts
"and that the true view. It's a new and harmless
"sort of craze, though you must be a forlorn body
"to have had it, for what if the ten newspapers took
"a true view of *you?* Have you no snug post, my
"friend? Have you never jobbed, filched, dispensed
"justice by the weight—have you nothing to fear
"from the hard glare of Truth being turned on
"your little proceedings? For remember" (and here
the Shadow grinned like the Lord Mayor over mar-

row puddings) "remember that if our ten news-
"papers agreed to speak out the truth there's not a
"stick or a stone of the many institutions you cherish
"which would be left standing. Think of that be-
"fore playing with the fire, and tell me who you
"are?"

"I am a clockmaker in a good way of business,"
responded the forlorn body suspiciously, "but I
"should like to know something about *you*." Then
the Shadow eyed him as a father might, and said:
"I am the ghost who haunts the *Times* office."

Now it is certain that a ghost haunts the *Times*
office, but whether it be that of the first Mr. J. Wal-
ter who founded our leading paper, or that of Captain Stirling, "The Thunderer," or that of honest
"toping Barnes," Mr. Delane's predecessor, has never
been ascertained. The clockmaker was not afraid
of ghosts, and this one in particular had nothing
unusual about him, except that when he stood in
the rays of the gas-light you could see through him
as if he were a tumbler of sherry. He bade the
clockmaker observe the transparency, for he was
anxious not to be set down for one who was trying
to pass himself off as a ghost without having any
right to the title. The clockmaker courteously declared that he had never doubted his word, and the

ghost having thanked him for this mark of confidence, proceeded:

"I have a personal interest in the realisation
"of your scheme, for I am doomed to wander
"about Printing-House Square until the day when
"the *Times* shall have spoken the truth, the
"whole truth, and nothing but the truth, in all
"its leaders, paragraphs, and correspondents' letters,
"for seven days in succession. I have waited years
"and years for my hour of release, but to speak
"with frankness I am not very sanguine of ever ob-
"taining it. Nevertheless I can help you and you
"me, for I have a few supernatural agencies at com-
"mand, and these agencies worked by living hands
"such as yours may procure us each what we desire
"—that is, to you the lively results that would ac-
"crue from universal veracity, to me a little un-
"broken sleep in the churchyard. Thus you say
"you are a clockmaker, and I'll be bound you pos-
"sess clocks 'warranted to keep good time——' "

"Aye, that I do," cried the clockmaker, proudly;
"plenty of clocks, big and small, that I'll back
"against any others in England."

"Just so," answered the ghost, not without a
doubting smile; "then our work will be so much
"the easier. Go you simply home and choose ten
"of your best clocks, regulate them, wind them up,

"and set them. On the day when they all mark
"the same time, strike the hours, half-hours, and
"quarters at exactly the same moment—no one of
"them being an instant before or behind the others
"—on that day the Spirit of Concord will be com-
"municated to the press of England; and there will
"flow from the newspaper offices such strong, har-
"monious strains of truth that abuses will vanish like
"icicles in the sun, and all we ghosts from Berwick
"or Land's End will hurry up to see the sport.
"Good night;" and with another dry laugh as if his
jaws stood more than ever in need of a little un-
guent, this ghost melted away.

The clockmaker hastened home, swept and
garnished a clean room on his top-floor, and carried
into it his ten best clocks. He knew them to be
good time-keepers, and set them of a row, some on
pedestals, some on the floor, according to their size;
and to each he affixed a label with the name of a
separate newspaper.

There was a big, solemn clock which professed
to tell everything—the quarter of the moon, the day
of the week and month, and which, moreover, had
a very variable barometer in its stomach, and this
one he called the *Times*. A smart, steady little
clock which struck loud and true without heeding
changes of weather or the vagaries of its com-

panions, he entitled *Pall Mall Gazette;* and a handsome drawing-room clock with gilt figures of footmen
in plush dancing minuets over it, he dubbed *Morning
Post.* The *Daily Telegraph* was of course represented
by a brazen clock on which were the words, "Greenwich time," and a brass bust showing Mr. Gladstone's
earnest features overhead*; and the *Daily News* and
Echo purported likewise to be guided by Greenwich,
though the former was surmounted by a fine statuette
of Miss Martineau in trousers, bearing a scroll with
the words "Woman's Rights;" and the latter was a
cheap clock of simile brass in *papier maché.* The
Standard, Globe, and *Morning Advertiser* had each
their special presentments, the last paper being sym-
bolised by a full-faced public-house clock, surmounted
by a 'scutcheon full of pewter measures and bottles.
They made a fine noise all ten together, but the
clockmaker little heeded that. He took his seat in
the centre of the room, holding his own chronometer
in his hand, and waiting anxiously for them all to
strike in harmony.

And he has been waiting ever since. If you
ever pass by the shop where this clockmaker resides,
walk straight up the steps and peer through the
keyhole as I did. You will find an unshaved man

---

* This was written when Mr. Gladstone was Premier.—Since then
tempora mutantur and *Telegraph* too.

with a bunch of clock-keys in one hand and a
piece of wash-leather with a bottle of oil in the
other. At times he shrieks and shakes his fist at
the clock marked *Telegraph;* but Mr. Gladstone's
earnest features remain unmoved, and the clock
strikes nine, ten, or eleven exactly as it suits it, and
without any reference to the real time of day. Oc-
casionally it will strike twelve, and the hour afterwards contradict itself by striking six; and the
papier mâché clock and the clock with the barometer
are both liable to the same complaint. As to the
full-faced clock, no power of invention has yet suc-
ceeded in making it strike eleven till full three-
quarters of an hour after that time has passed, and
the clockmaker has thrice pulled it to pieces and
thrice put it together again without inducing it to
amend. His eyes are standing out of his head like
cocoa-nuts in a shop window, and his ears have
lengthened. He sits a broken image of what he
once was, and has become a byword of reproach
amongst other clockmakers; but he is fired with a
holy zeal, and still hopes to succeed. When he
does I will write and tell you.

No. 9.—The Spade Guinea.

I HAVE thought much about currency and about payments in kind. A man who gave lessons on the drum, and who owed me seventy-four shillings, offered to settle the debt by drumming to me during seventy-four hours without stopping to eat or sleep. I preferred giving him a receipt in full; but if my debtor had been Madame Patti, who had volunteered to sit and sing to me for three days, even with occasional pauses for rest and refreshment, I might have deemed the arrangement reasonable—which proves that there is no laying down any absolute theories for one's rule and guidance.

I think, however, that there are anomalies in the kind and specie question which call for a remedy. The pawnshops will lend a man £5 on an inferior watch; but let him tender in pledge his superiorly-gifted mother-in-law and he will be unable to raise five shillings. Yet every law, moral and social, would compel a person to redeem his mother-in-law

at an early date.   He could not leave her to grow
dusty and moth-eaten in the warehouse.   To do so
would be to incur universal reprobation; but, granted
that he were wholly callous to the censure of his
contemporaries, the pawnbroker who had the mother-
in-law on his hands would still be compensated by
her intellectual companionship for the five shillings
which he had disbursed, so that no one would be
the loser.

I sometimes muse over these things in the Park,
remembering that we are a commercial people, but
that trade has not yet taken among us all the
developments which it might do.   Some of us have
many more relatives than we know what to do with,
whilst others go sorrowing for want of a noble-
hearted grandfather.   If those who had a few kinsfolk to spare could pass them over for a consideration to those who have none we should assuredly
be a happier people; though of course it would be
necessary to protect the purchasers against spurious
representations.   Thus any relative desirous of parting with Mr. Jenkins M.P. should be prohibited
from advertising him under one of those "grateful
"and comforting" labels used for Mr. Somebody's
cocoa.

This reminds me that fishing for trout one day
under Maidenhead Bridge I caught a piece of brown

paper. It got entangled in my hook, but just as I was about to restore it to the stream I felt it contained something hard, which proved to be a cardboard box containing a spade-guinea. Under the guinea lay a bit of paper from which I gathered that the guinea was not an ordinary one, for it would only consent to be expended on worthy objects. If its owner wished to lay it out in frivolous pursuits, in the encouragement of vain enterprises, or in the reward of undeserving individuals, the guinea melted in his fingers, though it would reappear faithfully in his waistcoat pocket by-and-by when the danger was over. Its last proprietor, who was a promoter of Enlightened British Liberalism—so said the paper— had tossed it furiously into the Thames after it had thrice refused to lend itself to a wholesale purchase of *Spectators* for dissemination among the benighted masses. He thought poorly of the guinea after this freak, and so did I; but I put it into my purse, then rolled up my fishing tackle and took the first train back to London, being minded to invest the queer coin as soon as possible.

The first man I met was a missionary bound for China with a cargo of rum and improving tracts. He asked me for a guinea, saying he was off to reform a heathen people, and recollecting the maxim about doing to others as you would be done by I

handed him my guinea without hesitation, for I have
long wished some Chinaman would come and reform us English. Two minutes afterwards I found
the piece of money inside my glove, and looking
back perceived the missionary peering about on the
pavement thinking he had dropped it down a drain.
I walked on and overtook a man who was hawking
songs in praise of the Great Liberal Party, and I
prepared to buy up the stock with the intention of
sending it to the London School Board. These
songs, as I reflected, would be just the things for
pauper children to warble in chorus instead of the
hymns which our progressive age has discarded as
denominational; but somehow my guinea fought as
shy of the cheap Government as it had done of the
missionary; and I was fain to proceed on my way
through town, trying very effectually every ten minutes
or so to dispose of my gold-piece.

I think I must have encountered fifty of my
honest countrymen bent on the promotion of different objects—political, religious, financial, and
scientific; and all declared that a spade-guinea
would be of great service to them. But the spade-
guinea declined to be serviceable. It melted over
the holes of subscription boxes, on counters, betwixt
fingers tinged with every shade of virtue and
patriotism; and ever it found its way back to my

pocket, where I began to dread it would stick fast
like a refractory gelatine ball. At last I remonstrated
with the coin, pulled it out, and gravely addressed
it; but in the course of my speech there came up to
me a smug sort of rogue with a disloyal face, who
said he wished to take out a patent for a new form
of laughing gas which would make the inhabitants
of these isles laugh and blurt out their thoughts im-
pulsively like those lost Frenchmen over the water.
I abominate patents, and do not believe in Frenchmen, so I gave the man my guinea, well knowing it
would revert to me before the rogue had vanished
round the corner. It did nothing of the kind, and
is still at large. I expect to see us all stricken with
mirth one of these mornings, though if we should
really take to laughing like the French what will
become of the many things and people whom you
and I could all name if it were not for the Law of
Libel?

No. 10.—References to Mr. Banting.

THE ball had been announced for ten o'clock, but he came at half-past eight the night before and sat down on the doorstep, liking to be punctual. They poured cold water on him from one of the upper windows, and the housemaids threw a cat at him from the area. Nothing could be more ingenious than the hints which the whole family gave to this too early guest to go away. But he wrung out the water from his clothes with both hands and kicked the cat; seeing which the family held a council about him in the dining-room, and ended by looking at him one after another over the blinds. They were a fat family, and it caused them uneasiness to see this lean man, who was tatooing with his heels quite comfortably as if he were minded to make a night of it.

Why was he thus lean when there were so many beeves about, and why did he let his hair flood over his shoulders when there are barbers enough who give one a Christian clip for sixpence? The upshot of it was that a footman was sent to invite him in to supper, and he turned out to be foreign—that is unused to the tongue of our people, having mistaken the cat for a British part of speech and the cold water for some of the liquid consonants. However he caught at the notion of a supper, and stalked with the pensive dignity of a wet man first into the house and then into the drawing-room.

The Christmas decorations were all ready. There was holly round the windows, round the looking-glasses, round everywhere, and a bunch of mistletoe, with berries of the usual surfeited complexion, hung from the chandelier. Also steams of food ascended from the kitchen; roast meats and stewed, puddings and spices clubbed their aromas, like flowers in a hot-house, and tickled the nostrils of the Fat Family, who spent a great deal of the day-time and most of the evening thinking of their nourishment.

There was Mabel and Rose, Florence and Angelina, whose dimpled chins and white teeth smiled at under-done meats and Burgundy; and Robert, Roderick, Richard and Reuben, who liked that a goose should be stuffed with chesnuts and that the porter at luncheon should have a creamy head. The

father and mother, both wheezy and venerable, were
not so stout as they once had been, but it was a
solace to them to reflect on the down-hill of life that
the lightest of their daughters weighed 14st. 12lb.
They were a thoughtful couple, who had protested
all their years against lean persons and who could
have no fellow-feeling with this particular lean man
whose clothes were damp and whose hair wanted
cutting. The drawing-room fire, too, roared at him.
A plethoric pug who belonged to Rose ran under
the table and barked; Mabel's Angora cat, and
Florence's parrot, whose perch was on the landing,
hissed and squalled each in his own style; and
Angelina's five gold fish put their noses against the
sides of their globe and wagged their gills with
a heavy derision at this singularly ill-favoured
man.

But he the while looked curiously at the piano
and strode towards it. The heat of the room was
drawing the moisture from his clothes in spiral
clouds which curled above his unkempt head, and
when he removed his gloves, of which he had
gnawed off the finger-tips during his meditation on
the doorstep, it was observed that his nails were
like fine bits of cowhorn. He sat down, touched
the keys of the instrument, laughed a quiet laugh—
which was remembered long afterwards to have been

one full of meaning—and began a set of quadrilles such as no man or woman had ever heard of. These quadrilles frightened the pug and the Angora cat down the staircase.

Up to this moment none of the Fat Family had spoken, deeming, in truth, that words would be wasted in trying to unravel a situation at once complex and disquieting. But at the first bar of music they started as if punctured with pins; at the second they clutched hold of the chairs and tables like people who are afraid of being carried away; at the third the furniture and they parted company, and, with reluctant and uncontrollable legs, the Fat Family began careering over the carpets.

Have you ever seen red-cheeked apples blown off a tree in a gale? Such were Mabel and Rose, Florence and Angelina, footing it with a vigour unequalled, yet against their will and with a breathless indignation, opposite Robert and Roderick, Richard and Reuben. The father and mother, who had thought to dance no more, uttered gasps of distress as they found themselves flinging their shoes at right angles with their ears; but worse than all was the predicament of the cook, butler, and three plump housemaids, who capered over the kitchen floor with the soup-tureens and salad dishes, the bowls, basins, and teacups—in short with all the things and people that were round-paunched and stood within ear-reach of the lean man's melody. .

For not only were the entire Fat Family stirred to motion. All down the streets sashes were thrown up and doors opened; each house poured out its contingent of fat tenants, whilst the lean ones craned out of the windows and watched them bound over the flags in the moonlight. Lord Justice James, who was passing that way, caught the sleekest policeman on the beat round his waist and spun with him among the lamp-posts until the beads rolled down their faces. In the dressing-rooms jugs and ewers clashed about over marble wash-hand stands, and in the bed-rooms pillows and bolsters rollicked over the counterpanes, whilst the thin fire-irons looked on amazed and rigid. Never was there such a night in the Calendar of the Fat. The news went abroad that a parish had caught fire; but there was no fire —it was only the Lean Man playing on the piano. Twenty times Robert and Roderick, Richard and Reuben panted to him to stop, but being un-used to the tongue of our people he only took this as a hint to play the faster, and clanged his cow-horn fingers on the keys with a redoubled energy.

Then the dancing ceased to have the aspect of anything human. Legs and arms flew to right and left like shirts and stockings hung out to dry in an east wind, the floorings groaned, all the loose bricks and slates were heard quadrilling on the roofs with the bulkier chimney pots, and the eyes of every living dancer jutted out of their sockets from the severity of this unwelcome exercise. The dancers also grew lean by perceptible degrees. The rumour came up that Lord Justice James and his policeman had galloped themselves to the spareness of thread-paper, and that many other corpulent people of note who had been drawn towards that street were losing flesh with a rapidity that was terrifying. It is certain, moreover, that all the obese persons in the county of Middlesex were fidgety that night, as if they felt that there was an agent about which put their substance in peril. Meanwhile the playing continued tempestuous and implacable, and it was not till three o'clock in the small hours that the Lean Pianist came to a sudden stop, after a final flourish which threatened to heave up the very houses.

During the last hour he had from time to time thrown quick glances over his shoulder like the shampooers in Turkish baths watching to see if the steam is operating, and only concluded when Mabel

and Rose, Florence and Angelina had dwindled to
the shadows of their former selves, whilst Robert and
Roderick, Richard and Reuben were holding up
their nether garments lest these useful clothes—now,
alas! many inches too big—should slip from them,
Then the pianist of evil rose, and, seeing his victims
strewn about the carpet with their tongues lolling,
he politely but firmly lifted up the Father of the
whilom Fat Family by the tails of his coat, and extracted from his pockets twenty shillings. This, said
he, in a speech understood of none, was his usual
fee, and in return for it he deposited a pack of
cards in the Father's shirt-front. These cards ran:
—"*Herr Teuffelsownrow, Inventor of the Utilitarian*
"*Music, and Pupil of Herr Wagner. References to*
"*Mr. Banting.*"

It is months ago since all this happened, and the
bemeagred family, with Lord Justice James and the
sleek policeman, have had time to grow fat again;
but the memory of the Lean Pianist haunts them
like a nightmare never to be forgotten. It was certainly he who had thinned Mr. Banting by dancing
him about Pall Mall in the dark,· but he had con-
strained that upholsterer under the stern threat of
fattening him again not to divulge the secret. He is
in London now and open to an engagement, having
taken out a patent for his music, which has the prop-

erty of ridding bodies animate and inanimate of their superfluities. Thus when the Fat Family had strength to look about them they discovered with consternation that not only they and their domestics had been reduced to lathes, but that their jugs and bowls had become spare cylinders, and that divers books and newspapers from which they had derived mental food had undergone transformations most piteous. Three-volume novels by eminent writers and writeresses, being ridden of their superfluous matter, had shrunk into the size of tracts; magazines stripped of their padding showed a drear account of empty pages; and a daily journal squeezed of all but the good sense in its columns was blank altogether.

It seems too that the Lean Pianist's music directed against Corporate Bodies, Town Councils, Parliaments, Cabinets, and the like, causes all useless members in them to melt away into smoke, which accounts for Herr Teuffelsownrow having never been invited to perform at Guildhall nor before her Majesty's faithful Commons. Nay, more, for Mr. Lowe having fears lest this man should ever come with flute and pipe in Downing Street has been brooding his suppression, though, seeing that we are a free people who cannot be molested without a pretext, the Home Secretary will not punish Herr Teuffels-

ownrow for simply playing music. He will get him
dealt with him for diminishing Lord Justice James
in contempt of the Court of Appeal.

No. 11.—"Silly Billy."

IN a night of hilarity between a bottle of claret and two of port, all three empty, was written the unique tale of *"Silly Billy."* The author's pen flew over the sheets and the sheets flew over the table; when the final chapter had been brought to a close by a blot the man went off with his work, hot as a pancake or a colonel's temper, to the first publishing firm reputed solvent. A month later "Silly Billy," printed on post octavo with wide margins to make the public think they had got more of it, came out and was read with mingled feelings, chiefly peppery.

Till then the author had been a quiet man, collecting postage-stamps and matching wools for his grandmother. He had frequently done his duty as a Christian by renouncing the devil's works on behalf of squealing infants whom he had never seen before nor was likely to see again, and he carried an umbrella like the rest of us, because of the climate.

When "Silly Billy" appeared he was the foremost to read it, and he pronounced it a good book until he remembered he was the author, which set him wondering, for he was a just reasoner, who felt that the credit lay quite as much with the three bottles—one of claret and two of port—as with himself. Alone he could not have imagined such a work. When he came to consider the chapters he perceived in this passage the spirit of port, in that other the promptings of claret; but nowhere could he discover traces of his own mind's work. There were even paragraphs which he disapproved on principle, for he had many principles, so that, stimulated at last by conscientious prickings, he wrote to the publishers and suggested an *erratum* stating, *"This book was "dictated by Three Bottles to a writer who objects to "some of it."* But the publishers preferred leaving him the undivided honour, whereupon this man experienced a sensation as of having defrauded somebody whom he loved, and his features lengthened, to the great distress of his grandmother whose wools he used to match. The book, meanwhile, was selling. Some people read it twice, others who could not read wished they could for "Silly Billy's" sake, and the author began to taste the toothsome fruits of popularity.

A few actions for libel were brought against him.

In the universal sensitiveness which a widespread self-consciousness of respectability begets, no man can read of a ragamuffin without musing, "Why, here "am I, drawn to the life!" The claimants to the character of "Silly Billy" were numerous and convinced. More than one person in eminent station said:—"Silly Billy can only be meant for me," and at this all his friends chorussed like one single friend: "Yes indeed, Silly Billy can only be meant for "you!"

Pall Mall became hot to the *collaborateur* of the three bottles, and Piccadilly was an avenue of grief to him. He sought to explain; but explanations never disturb facts, and it was a fact that Silly Billy's head-dress fitted a number of discreet and pious folks quite comfortably. That version about the bottles did not mend the author's case either, for though three bottles may advise a man to throw himself off London Bridge, say tender things to a well-seasoned widow, or make a speech without head or tail, it is absurd to ascribe to them any talents for literature. So said many critics who were connoisseurs on the subject, and the author of "Silly "Billy" was fain to closet himself in his dining-room, where face to face with the empty three bottles which he had fetched up from the cellar, he upbraided them for the unmannerly trick they had played him.

It was a lop-eared scene, full of bitterness on the one side, and of cynical unconcern on the other, for the cabs as they rattled outside caused the bottles to jingle, and the burden of this jingle of theirs was "Silly Billy, Silly Billy!" No man can be expected to stand nonsense when it does not agree with him, and in a moment of electric fluidism the author pitched the three bottles into the fender, then rushed from his dining-room a baffled, disappointed man.

He addicted himself to toast-and-water, matching wools more conscientiously than before, and stuck postage-stamps in an album from sunrise to midnight. A young lady who espied him from a window opposite took a gradual interest in his work. She was a sweet, good girl, who devoted much of her time to intellectual pursuits, watching her guardian dot-and-carry-one on a high stool. Her eyes were hazel, her pretty hair frizzled over her brow like a poodle's, and she had a well-founded belief in orange-fritters. To her this man made love. Two Japanese stamps wrapped in lead paper proved to her the depth of his affection; when he parted for her sake with the only negro stamp he possessed, she saw that he was a man who would go to the length of any sacrifice. All that remained for him to do was to marry her and tell his name; but he

did the last thing first, and then she smiled an arch
smile, and exclaimed,

"Why, it's the name of the man who wrote 'Silly
"Billy;' are you relatives?"

"Yes," sighed he, raising her fingers to his lips;
"yes, and good friends too, for it was I who wrote
"'Silly Billy;'" but he had no space to add something witty, as he had intended to do, for the rosy
hand was whisked out of kissing reach and fell seven
or eight times upon his ears, making a noise as if
leather was being thwacked. Up jumped the guardian meanwhile, off his high stool, flung his heaviest
ruler at the man, and screamed in a paroxysm that
rift all the kitchen milk-pails into bits, "Ah! you've
"the face to come here after writing that lampoon
"on me!" And the man had only time to roar,
"Give me back my Japanese stamps!" when he was
bundled into the street with ignominy.

A sad monk was passing that way looking for a
cab. He was an erudite man, whose hair was never
brushed by machinery, for he shaved it every Saturday night with a shilling razor; but he had a lenient
soul under his unwashed face, and he said to the
author whom he met in this pickle, "Come into the
"cab with me; you shall pay half the fare." The
author complied. There were moments when he
showed the meekness of a lamb, besides which he

knew that he should not pay half the fare, for he
made a point of always leaving his purse at home.

The cab, going at a sensible pace, took them to
Wandsworth or Islington, and the monk conversed
about monastic rules, dry bread, hair shirts, and
other topics calculated to raise the flagging spirits of
his companion. Between whiles he sang snatches of
the Penitential Psalms, in a fervent bellowing voice
that shook the cab and caused the driver to hold on
by the box-rail for fear of falling off; and all this
melted the author's heart, so that he murmured,
"Why should not I too be a monk? My hair is
"nothing to me, and boots have ever been my ab-
"horrence."

Saying which, he perceived that the cab had
reached a gate and passed it, and now they set eyes
on a number of other chaste monks cultivating their
minds by planting cauliflowers in parallel rows. A
curfew was tolling. The wind blew, rain was patter-
ing against the monastery walls, everything spoke of
peace and blessedness, and the friar, after an impressive rebuke to the author for evading his share
of the cab hire, led him by the cuff through half a
mile of damp passages into the cell of the Father
Superior, a man of saintly gauntness, who looked as
if he were waiting for the dinner-bell.

There the author found rest at last, a patient

ear, and hard bricks to kneel on whilst he poured
out the full confession of his tortured soul. He told
all about the three bottles; he made no effort to
conceal that two of them were port and one claret,
both dry wines high in flavour; and he was dilating
on the tribulations of "Silly Billy" when the Superior
sprang up with every bristle of his baize gown
standing on end, and both eyes glaring like a spotted
hyæna's. He clutched the penitent by his necktie,
shook him like a bag of linen for the washerwoman,
and thunderingly shouted, "It's you, then, inky worm!
"who've been the bane of my holy life! What had
"I done to you that you should pourtray me to a
"world of heathens as 'Silly Billy'?"

"But I didn't!" shrieked the penitent in his
desperate struggles for breath.

"Ah! falsehood allied to impudence! Come and
"listen to your doom!" howled the Superior; and
flinging open the cell-door he dragged the author
by the scruff, down stone steps, up corridors, under
vaults, bumping, thumping, and kicking him with
sandals to a crypt where five hundred monks—the
duskiest in these isles—were sitting on their heels
and yelling in a major key of intense heartiness:—

Maledictus ille qui
Male scripsit, hei mihi!
"*Stultum, stultum Gulielmum!*"

"This is too much to be borne!" raved the author, and he fled into the kitchen-garden. The monks flung cauliflowers after him, the curfew raised a hue and cry, the Brotherhood's bull-dog was let loose, and the author as he clambered over the wall left the larger part of his most necessary garments on the spikes.

What more shall we add? The man of mind rises superior to misfortune, and this one rose to the height of six foot two. He visited foreign climes, was shot at in Madrid, eaten by mosquitoes at Rome, blown up in a Mississippi steamer, and sued for damages for obstructing the atmosphere, by the enlightened democracy who lived on the river shores. In process of time he took a ticket home, and arrived in St. James's Street as the lampmen were lighting the gas. But he was not prepared for the adventures that followed. An old enemy who saw him from a club window dropped a glass of sherry-and-bitters, rushed out, and danced round him, halloaing: "Silly Billy's dead—old Thingamy, you "know, whom you touched off in that book! Come "and liquor up! It's the best thing that was ever "written." Another scuttled across the road with his boot-laces untied and clamoured: "Dinner with my "family to-morrow! Uncle What's-his-name — the "man you meant for Silly Billy—never got over your

"book: it killed him like a gun, and I was his heir.
"My wife blesses you ever." A third hastened up,
then a fourth, a fifth, a twenty-seventh, and an
eighty-ninth, till the club staircase was black with
them and the author's experienced arms became
loose in their sockets; for they patted him on the
back, helped him to clear soup, whistled him the
"Silly Billy Waltz" composed in his absence by
Coldstream Godfrey, and introduced the Chief Com-
missioner of Works, who took his measure for a
cheap statue.

Nothing indeed could exceed the festiveness of
that memorable evening, and last of all the little
woman who loved orange fritters arrived also, saying: "I have the licence in my pocket and we'll be
"married next week at twelve. Those boxes on the
"ear you received couldn't have hurt you, and now
"my guardian and I have both forgiven you, for we
"are convinced 'Silly Billy' was only an autobio-
"graphy."

Big Ben itself rang the chimes for that auspi-
cious betrothal and everything occurred as suggested.
The Sad Monk—now washed and promoted to
superiorship, *vice* the other superior hurried by
"Silly Billy" into a lasting sleep—came and performed the wedding rite, and the five hundred
dusky monks stood in the organ-loft and chanted

their new canticle, "Benedictus ille qui bene "scripsit," &c. Nor was this all; for twelve months after there was a christening, at which Mr. Gladstone and Mr. F. C. Burnand officiated as sponsors, and as the party were setting out for church Mr. Gladstone had a happy thought. Said this great man with an earnest smile: "We will christen him "'Silly Billy'"; but Lord Shaftesbury, who was present, and had put on a cowl and sandals to assist the monk in his ministrations, had a thought still happier, and added piously: "We will each "drink three bottles in his honour, two of port and "one of claret."

No. 12.—The Seven Highlanders of Ben-Haggis.

THERE were seven Highlanders from Ben-Haggis who lived on an attic-floor overlooking Finsbury Park, and wore red hair and beards so as not to seem ashamed of their national colours. The reddest had been steeped in low spirits from his infancy; the other six were sorry over their meals from thinking how Charles I. had died. As was to be expected, the esteem of Finsbury followed them both on the way to their daily place of business and in their Sunday walks, for they voted on Mr. Torrens's side at election time, and carried photographs of Sir Andrew Lusk under their flannel waistcoats to cheer them in hungry moments.

They also delighted the whole quarter with their music. When they sat down seven of a company to play their bagpipes, in a room which had been built for five, the kettle boiled with the heat of their performance; and the one who could blow away for an hour after the others had left off earned a sheep's-

7*

head. In their relations they were brotherly. Their shirt-collars, hats, and moral precepts were in common; each man swore by the one who sat next him, and sometimes they all swore at one another. Of the gifts that go to make up strong, simple, red-headed men, these seven were possessed; and it was natural that, being so united in mind, they should blend the affections of their hearts likewise on one common object. This they did by all seven proposing marriage to the same woman.

Her name was Zoe, and she kept the glove-shop in King Street. If there be a glove-shop in King Street we do not mean that one, but the one next door. Zoe's every-day attire was a dress of grey pearl silk trimmed with sky-blue; she sported a black velvet ribbon round her neck with a turquoise locket, and at her breast a turquoise brooch, shaped like a bunch of forget-me-nots. These forget-me-nots had much to do with the firm trade of the shop, for, ogling Zoe's brooch, customers neglected to see whether their gloves fitted; and, when the gloves took to cracking at the corner of Piccadilly, the wearers returned with a deep immutable purpose, to buy fresh pairs. The Highlanders, having never bought gloves, were not likely to begin on learning that the price of these superfluities had risen to five-and-sixpence; but they came one night after tea

and hallooed the mountain ballads of their country
till they brought out all the men from White's and
Boodle's, the spectators from the theatre over the
way, and the people reading books at the London
Library, Afterwards arrived the police, and Zoe
laughed at the scene through her window; but the
next morning each of the Highlanders received a
note on cream-laid paper inviting him to call in
King Street at a stated hour the same evening.

They were punctual to this appointment, though
it was their dinner-time, and they would rather have
come later; but Zoe greeted them with a friendly
smile, and on the counter of her small shop, per-
fumed with amber and violet, they beheld two pairs
of gloves—one preternaturally large, the other tiny
beyond compare. The big gloves—technically they
must have been "fifteens"—could only have fitted
the most large-handed man in this kingdom—say
Mr. Lowe; the small ones would have been almost
too tight even for the Countess of D—— or Miss
M—— W——, the actress.

"And now," said Zoe, turning the gloves over
with her own little hands, which sparkled with the
fire of jewelled rings, "now nothing obliges me to
"marry one of you, and I have vowed by the most
"precious thing I have, which is an annuity in the
"Three per Cents., that I will not belong to any

"man who cannot wear one of these two pairs of
"gloves when he takes me to the church opposite
"the Moore and Burgess Minstrels."

This is what Zoe said, sprinkling some powder
into the gloves to give the Highlanders every chance.
But these seven men circled round the counter with
beetling looks, examining the gloves, and from that
moment there was strife between them. Why conceal that five of them, after bestowing on the matter
two minutes of attentive thought, gave up the
struggle, and emigrated a week later to the free
lands of Muskoka, where they have been pulling up
stumps ever since, to the pride and comfort of their
friends at Ben-Haggis? The other two remained
face to face with the gloves, and with a purpose of
settled hostility. The better to mark the complete
divergence of their views from that day forth, one
dissented from the Established Kirk, and went to
live on the north side of the Strand; the other subscribed to the Turkish baths, and took lodgings on
a line with Somerset House. The name of the first
of these rivals was McFinn, and of the second
McFunn. If there be two Scotchmen of these names
hating each other in the Strand we retract all that
has been said, for we are not going to have anyone
calling in Tavistock Street for explanations.

McFinn was the Highlander who had been

steeped in low spirits, and, having an earnest mind, he resolved that he would try and make his hands grow so as to fit the big gloves. To this end he borrowed them of Zoe, and hung them over his chimney-piece, partly as ornaments, partly in the hope that the smoke might shrink them—which it never did. Then McFinn embarked on a course of all those pursuits that conduce to large-handedness. He sent half his income to the Chancellor of the Exchequer as "conscience money," and subscribed 3s. 6d. every Sunday to pay off the National Debt, As a means of encouraging the Post-Office he put five stamps on his letters where one would have done, and dropped postage-cards by the dozen into the main sewer. Not a day passed without his attending Westminster Hall and the Parliament lobbies to see whether the eminent people there stood in need of any present; and, having taken his notes, he sent Mr. T. Collins a new hat, Mr. Auberon Herbert a new yellow coat, Mr. W. E. Forster, Lord Spencer, and the Bishop of Manchester each a razor, Mr. T. B. Potter, Mr. Dalglish, and Sir W. W. Wynn Mr. Banting's book and a bag of rusks a-piece, the Duke of Somerset and Mr. Stansfeld some curling-tongs, and Lord Charles Russell, Mr. Justice Hawkins, and Lord Halifax some hair-oil.

Nor did his benevolence stop here, for he was

aware that there is generosity of the soul as well as
of the purse, so he lavished all the treasures of his
intellect on those who were deficient. He spent his
nights hunting up rhymes for Lord Houghton, and
forwarded them to him by telegraph. He gave
thoughtful advice to Mr. Gladstone on bits of paper
dropped into his letter-box, hints for universal
letters in the *Times* to Sir William Harcourt, also
Latin quotations to spice them withal, maxims on
truthfulness to Mr. S. Lefevre, all the jocularity he
could spare — it was not much, but a man does
what he can—to Mr. Jacob Bright and the Duke of
Argyll, to be divided between them, and his blessing
to every person he met.

But for all this his hands did not broaden across
the palms; nay, it is painful to state they diminished.
Every night after he had passed a daytime in good
works he sat on his bed—the only article of furniture left him, for he had given away his chairs,
tables, and fire-irons to help to furnish the new law-
courts—and he essayed to believe that the gloves
fitted better than the night before. One evening,
however, he thrust his head into the left-hand glove
by mistake, and it fell over his ears; whereat he recognised that his illusions were as vain as the line
of rail that was to carry our brave Fantees into
Coomassie.

There was no doubt his mode of life was thinning the man. He never dined without insisting that the waiter should take a chair and eat half his soup out of the same plate; and when potatoes and brocoli were served him he made two portions of them, and carried the larger to the hungriest neighbour he could set eyes on. These things play havoc with a Christian, and McFinn found no solace but in his bagpipes, which he had determined to send as a present to the Duke of Edinburgh, and on which he piped meanwhile with a fireful sadness which troubled all the skeletons in the churchyards of St. Clement-Dane's and St. Mary-le-Strand, and all the night charges in Bow Street. When his melodious instrument had gone to Gloucester House McFinn set off for King Street, and said, "These "gloves will never do for me, Zoe." But cruel Zoe, who was selling a bottle of *Jockey Club*, some smoking pastilles, a betting-book, and two pairs of buff dogskins, red seamed, to Dr. Cumming—Zoe answered with a toss of the head, "If the big gloves "don't fit you then exchange with McFunn, who has "got the small ones."

So McFinn went in search of McFunn, and discovered him taking exercise in the red-hot room at the Hammam, Jermyn Street. McFunn had sought to reduce himself by steam, and had meditated over all the devices by which men grow close-fisted. There was no precious thing ever came in his way but he clutched at it, hugged it, stored it, and his cupboards were full of valued tracts by Lord Stratford de Redcliffe, unredeemed pledges of the great Liberal Party, and locks of hair of all the ladies on the provincial school-boards. With these treasures nothing would induce McFunn to part. His principles were to claim thirteen-pence when he asked change for a shilling; and to mop up the gravy in his plate with a piece of bread so that no one in the kitchen should profit. But he had not become lean on the system; over-indulgence in precious things had swollen his fingers to twice their original size, and he would have shed tears had he not made it a habit to waste nothing. He and McFinn eyed each other in that hot-room, but when McFunn guessed that McFinn wished to take his opinion on the altered sizes of their fingers, then he clenched his teeth and howled, for he clung to his opinion as he did to everything else; and McFinn, who was always giving, gave tongue forthwith, so that they were both bundled into the street and their clothes thrown out to them through a window.

It was at this unexpected moment, when the earth seemed bleakest to them, that looking up as he drew on his boots, McFinn espied Mr. Baxter

and Mr. Rylands coming down the street arm-in-
arm with some Yorkshire hams from Fortnum and
Mason's and with each other. Now, excepting Mr.
Lowe, who more large-handed in this kingdom than
Mr. Baxter, late of the Admiralty, who saved our coals
for us at the expence of our ships? McFinn posted
after this regretted public servant, drew him up the
nearest mews, and steadfastly appealed to him to
try on the big gloves. Mr. Baxter, though surprised—he is a man of surprises—wedged his ham
cautiously between his knees, tried on the gloves,
and wanted to walk off with them, for they fitted him.

Then McFinn said, "The gloves are yours, but
"on condition only of your dressing up like me,
"putting on a hair and a beard like me, and passing
"yourself off for me at the glove-shop round the
"corner."

"You'll pay for the wig?" queried Mr. Baxter,
eyeing the gloves with a careful eye.

"I will, and you shall keep it," answered the
generous Scotchman, whose wit and liberality brought
him in a golden return, for Mr. Baxter did faithfully as he was bidden, and won him the hand of
Zoe.

The marriage came off in due course—it was
Mr. Baxter who figured at the altar, but he and
McFinn changed places after the ceremony—and

now McFinn keeps the glove-shop in King Street, where we have written this true narrative at his dictation, and with Zoe at our elbow to correct faults in spelling.

And now we have only to warn all and any such who may feel ruffled at being mentioned herein, that we have borrowed a cat from the *Guardian* office, and he shall protect us.

No. 13.—The Purse.

EVERYONE has come to the reflection that the happiness of a man's life resembles a small piece of butter spread over a large slice of bread; and the rest of the people have thought of it as of one ration of beef between six men. It is a fact that we always get less of it than we can eat, and, what is better, the little of it there is seldom lights on one at the right moment. A man who knew these things, but had written them down on his hat-lining for greater convenience in the remembering, had taken to making such a noise against Destiny that Destiny ended by having enough of him. It appeared to the clamourer under the form of a clerk of sober years, and requested him to put down his complaints on paper in the usual way, with stops and points of exclamation where they were needed. This he did during two nights and a day, omitting nothing of the bits of luck that had befallen him when he was past using them — such as a tor-

toiseshell comb sent him when all his top hair was
gone — and he concluded by averring that if he
could dispose of his happiness as he pleased, making
it turn up when wanted, just unlike a cab in the
suburbs, he should have nothing more to say.
Having signed this he slept on it, and next morning when he awoke found a red silk purse on his
table, and under the purse a paper with some
smudged printing on it like the frank on a Government clerk's love-letters.

This is what the paper said:—

"Disagreeable Sir,—Destiny having given your
"complaints her attentive consideration, desires to
"be well rid of you from this day. You were en-
"titled, like some other persons, to a fixed revenue
"of happiness, payable in daily or weekly instalments
"according to circumstances; but Destiny cheerfully
"consents to commute this pension into a lump sum,
"which you will find in the accompanying purse.
"Each of the gold coins in that purse represents a
"certain modicum of felicity; and, that you may fully
"understand your altered position, you will do well
"to make note of the following instructions:—

"1. The gold coins stand for large pieces of
"happiness; but as every great joy comprises a num-
"ber of small ones, the gold can be changed for
"silver or copper luck-money.

"2. The way to obtain change is to ring a gold "piece on the table, crying 'Change!' and the result "of this will be twenty silver pieces; the silver coins, "handled in the same manner, will each yield twelve "bits of copper.

"3. To spend a coin you must fling it out of "the window, wishing, as you do so, for something "within reason. You are not entitled to anything "unreasonable, and, if you were to wish all your "hair to grow again, that would be an immoderate "request which could on no account be granted.

"4. If you throw away a coin without wishing, "you will simply receive one of the instalments of "happiness which it had been intended you should "get in due course; but you will get it at once.

"5. The coins are transferable, and the persons "to whom you may give them will be entitled to "the happiness funded for you, or to whatever "good thing (within reason, as before) you may wish "them.

"6. When you have spent all the coins you will "find no more where they came from.

"I feel no honour in subscribing myself
"Your humble servant,
"THE CLERK OF DESTINY."

When the man had imbued himself with the
sense of this paper, he laid it down and tarried little
before throwing up his window-sash. Despite his
hairlessness—which was due not to age but to the
fermentation of useful thoughts within him—he was
an eager man, much addicted to seeing that all
things concerning him worked comfortably. The
coins he fingered were heavy, well struck, stamped
with the word "Luck;" and he flung one of them
straight out of the window, wishing that Mr. Gladstone and his Cabinet might sail for the Gold Coast
and put an end to the fighting there by their genius.
This was not an unreasonable request, and a third
edition of the *Times* which was bawled in the streets
an hour later announced that the Ministers were
busy packing, but would be put through their bayonet
exercise that afternoon in the yard of the War Office
by Mr. Cardwell.

This was pleasure enough for one day to a man
who took but a subdued interest in politics—just
the interest which a grass-blade takes in a roller—
and so the owner of the purse restored the coins to
his pocket, and went out for a walk Kensington-
wards, for he was in love with someone who lived
that way. It was, in truth, more than love, for there
was a question of banns in it, only complicated by
the doubt as to whether the two parties suited each

other. They both had complained tartly of Destiny, both had quiet tempers of their own, and both had written letters of protest to the newspapers against the adulteration of tea, mustard, and cocoa-nibs. When the man reached Kensington he pondered with the knocker in his hand as to whether he would tell Almie — for her name was Alma — about the purse in his coat-tail; but he decided he would not. His soul's peace was to be so much dependent upon her moods that it occurred to him as a subtle inspiration that if he disbursed his money in keeping Almie always smiling there might be an end to his perplexities present and to come. Moved by this thought he let go the knocker and drew the purse to buy some smiles there and then. But here a query arrested him: what was the worth of a smile of Almie's?—was each one valuable at gold or copper? To do the man full justice he rated the smiles so high—having seen few of them by reason of a certain curate who had more top-knot than he—that he was for parting with a handful of the gold to ensure a week's smiles, and at this pace would have drained his purse before the month was out. But he was spared this extravagance by Almie coming to the door before he had yet opened the purse's mouth. She was blooming with smiles—unbought smiles, most springlike and refreshing—and she greeted him with an air of mystery, as if there was something nice for dinner.

There was nothing nice except herself, for the cook attended a School of Scientific Cookery with many other cooks and some troopers in the Blues, and had little time to waste on the mere practice of her profession; but the warmth in Almie's eyes atoned for the lack of it in the soup, and the air of mystery she wore continued from course to course as if the something nice would come after all if one only had the patience to wait for it. And now watch the change that stole over the whole nature of the man with the purse. He had been a fractious subject, querulous on account of his top hair, and ferocious towards the lesser clergy whenever he saw that curate above-mentioned turn the treadle of Almie's sewing-machine, and take a lesson from her in hemming his own pocket-handkerchiefs—the animal!

But after that memorable evening at which the something nice never turned up—not even at tea-time, though the man looked for it under the toast and Sally-luns—his life began to flow as unaccountably smooth as Mr. Grant-Duff's self-praises during recess. He spent no money from his luck-purse, and yet Almie beamed more and more every

day, like a little silver tea-pot—she was not unplump
—in the sunlight. She had gushing outbursts of
playfulness, amiability, solicitude; she read up leaders
in the *Spectator* to amuse him of an evening, nor did
she fail to cry with him for a gentle half-an-hour
over the unkindness of men who accused Mr. Gladstone of being a rampageous old woman; and all this
disturbed the financial plans which the man had
formed for the expenditure of his luck-coins. Seeing
there was no need, for the present at least, of in-
vesting them in Almie's smiles, he had bethought
him of waiting till the curate appeared again, and
then flinging a copper coin—if necessary a silver
one—out of the window every morning to get him
out of the way. But the curate did not appear again,
having taken to his bed on account of the decline
of Rugby, and having been ordered a change of
climate to Madeira along with two hundred and
sixteen other pupils of Dr. Temple's similarly afflicted
with *cerebro-Haymaniasis*. In despite of this, though,
Almie smiled and smiled like any Frenchwoman at
a Female Rights meeting, and the man with the
purse, convinced that his money was becoming useless so far as his domestic bliss was concerned,
of associating himself in some way with the public
happiness, as he had done when he sent Mr. Gladstone to the Gold Coast.

He could not forget the pleasurable emotions of the multitudes who pressed their faces through the railings of the War Office yard and watched Popular William go through his platoon drill with a wicker helmet on his thoughtful head—the very statue of Sidney Herbert had turned round to lose nothing of the manly sight—and accordingly he launched himself for some days on a course of reckless outlay for the common good. Let it be added that he took care to wish for nothing unreasonable as he jerked his coins out of the window and looked at their melting like snow-flakes before they reached the pavement.

In wishing that *Punch*, so comic with its funeral odes, might become a grave paper again, with Dean Close to edit it—in desiring that Cremorne might become a tea-garden with Mr. Barrow and the Licensing Justices of Middlesex for its constant customers —in praying that the Railway Interest in Parliament might be solaced for their great grief over smashed expresses by inheriting all the chattels of their victims—he coveted nothing out of honest reason, and his requests were fulfilled to the letter, as we have all of us had occasion to see. Only once did he give proof of unreason, and that was in flinging a gold piece into space in order that the reviewers might take to reading the works they criticised; but as these unfortunates have but a week allowed them wherein to judge some two dozen books, this was as immoderate as wishing that an Attorney-General might read all the briefs for which he gets paid, and so the precious gold piece was wasted.

But now, all of a sudden, a curious twist occurred in the purseman's life—a twist which proves the power of love. In disposing of his coins to the end that you and we might sleep the sound sleep of the just and unjust, he had forgotten that Almie might, at some distant day when years had made her plumper but less smileful, be glad of the luck-money he was now frittering so prodigally. What, too, if underneath her smiles lurked some present little troubles unavowed? Women have been known to smile like angels when boots pinched them, stays racked them, and towering chignons made their poor tiny heads split—then why not when moral stays or other such sufferings ground their hearts into powder? It is only a matter of love for the man they may fancy, and the owner of the purse felt himself to be lovable—irresistible indeed, notwithstanding his hair. But when these thoughts flashed upon him you should have seen the desolation of his countenance; nothing could beat it except the face of Mr. Ayrton going to draw the salary of a sinecure of which he disapproves on

principle. Quick as impulse the man took a cab
to Kensington, sprang up the steps, was admitted,
and ran into the drawing-room, where Almie, with a
monogram paper before her, was admiring the coats-
of-arms of the banker-barons, for she had ever been
fond of curiosities. The man took her hands, and,
so doing, mutely soliloquised, "Almie and I will be
"married by that Rugby man as soon as he feels
"better, and what use are these coins to me so long
"as she smiles like that? The coins are for her.
"I want to be sure that her smiles are genuine, and
"will last all this year, next year, and following
"years." Saying which he encircled Almie's waist
with his arm, and took an easy opportunity of dropping his purse into her little pocket.

It was a splendid dinner that evening, for the
cook, returning from her Scientific Academy towards
seven, found time to broil a chop or two, and the
kitchen-maid, who knew nought of science, contrived a pudding. But, O Prodigy! for when the
man wended his way homewards at the starry time
of night he felt something weighing down his coat-
pocket, and, pausing under a lamp-post to recon-
noitre the mystery, he drew out a parcel wrapped
in silver paper, and inscribed in Almie's writing—
"*This is my wedding present.*" He opened it, and
unveiled a purse like his own—only bright blue in-

stead of red—and chokefull of all the luck-money which was to have lasted Almie for a life-time. For she, too—brave little woman—had had high words with Destiny, and she too had seen her pension commuted on the terms hereinbefore mentioned. A policeman, who found the favoured man blubbering under a lamp-post at the dead of night, took him to the station, and charged him with being drunk and disorderly; and the next day one of our acute stipendiary magistrates fined him five shillings and gave him a caution.

No. 14.—The Promising Candidate.

THIS is a tale about three candidates whom the Dissolution flung into the express train which leaves London in the morning for Swallowburgh. Their names were Dumple, Crumple, and Thumple, and they travelled in separate carriages. Crumple was the ladies' man, and stood for a free tea-table, with plenty of clergy round it; Dumple was for a free beer-barrel; and Thumple was for squashing the other two. The "Lamb" was the place that housed Crumple; Dumple hired the best rooms at the "Buck"; and Thumple made a speech out of the window of the "Red Lion" before he had changed his linen. From the outset ale and stout began to flow at the expense of Dumple and Crumple, because there was to be no bribery or corruption; and Thumple chartered an agent to join in the drinking, and take notes about it. Eleven boys with tattered trousers pasted bills on the walls expounding all that Dumple thought; squealing cohorts of ladies with spectacles strode about the streets with a banner in honour of Crumple; and when it was suggested to Thumple that he should wet his throat with some brandy-and-water before he began to spout again he jumped seven feet high at the notion.

Now there was staying in the town an individual to whom we alluded on a former occasion—none other than the Man with the Glass Eye. He had snatched many secrets from Nature, and seeing Dumple, Crumple, and Thumple hurry under his windows, he mused about them as he buttered the toast which his landlady had sent up. No one was admitted to his musings, but on the day before the nomination this man went to the Town Hall, where the Mayor and Common Council were sitting round a table and calling each other names for want of something more amusing to do. One third of the Council were for Thumple, the next third would hear nothing against Crumple, and the last third— among whom was the Mayor—fancied there was most to say for Dumple, and said it because there was a great deal of sherry in them. The Man with the Glass Eye had no right in the council-room, but he took the right of walking steadily up to the Mayor's left hand, and offering a few remarks. "After all," said he, laying a small wire box on one

of the blotting-books, "what you want is to find the
"best man." "He's going to speak for Dumple,"
cried the Mayor, at which two-thirds of the Council
stood up, and bawled, "Turn him out!" But the
man replied, "Dumple is no more to me than
"Crumple or Thumple." Whereupon the Mayor and
his third shouted as if the sherry was troubling
them, "You've no business here; go downstairs and
"look at the pump."

The pump was a great institution in Swallowburgh, and everybody was proud of it—especially
the milkmen; but the Man with the Glass Eye had
tried it now and then, and, all things considered, he
preferred his whisky neat. As a means of restoring
quiet, he brought down his foot with a bang on the
table, and halloaed,

"You shall all have some more sherry if you
"hold your tongues"; and after this they sat so still
you might have heard their beards grow. "Now it
"comes to this," proceeded the man, wiping the
mark of his foot off the table with the tail of the
Mayor's gown; "who's the best candidate? Why
"the man who makes most promises. "And who's
"the next best? Why the man who keeps them.
"It follows, then, that if you could get hold of a
"candidate who would both make promises and
"keep them, he would be like the Phœnix."

"Who's Phœnix?" interrupted the Mayor, in a
suspicious tone. "No connection of yours," rejoined
a Councillor who held for Thumple; but he was
forced to go on his knees with his nose in the dust
and apologise, for the Councillors might call one
another names, but not use personalities. "I wish
"to say now," continued the speaker, "that I have
"something in this box which will force your new
"member to keep his promises. As soon as the
"election is over the Mayor will go up to the re-
"turned burgess and pat him kindly on the back;
"then, touching the spring of this lid, he will hand
"him the box, saying, 'Here's a gift that will pre-
"vent you from forgetting your friends at Swallow-
"burgh.'"

"It's Crumple who'll win the box," bellowed a
Councillor who squinted.

"No, it's Thumple," roared another, wagging his
ears in defiance; whereat these two caught each
other by the hair, and the last heard of them was
as they rolled down the staircase one on the top of
the other, carefully refraining from any but Parliamentary adjectives. The Town. Clerk entered a
minute of the proceeding, but the Mayor, who never
forgot himself, laid hold of the Man with the Glass
Eye, and muttered, "You promised us some sherry!"

"Come and have it," answered the man, generously. "We'll go to the 'Buck,' the 'Lamb,' and the "'Red Lion'; you shall have three half-pints a-piece, "and tell Dumple, Crumple, and Thumple of what "we've been planning for them." So said and so done. It was past midnight when two policemen brought home the Mayor in a wheel-barrow and rang for his wife to let him in. "Dumple's the man "who'll win the box!" hiccoughed his worship whilst they laid him on the mat; but his wife, as she helped him up to bed with a broomstick, could be heard vociferating, "You'll vote for Crumple, who "stands for the teapot! Crumple's my man! "Crumple!"

It was Thumple, however, who headed the poll. He spoke from Monday at daybreak till the hour for closing the public-houses on Saturday, and he was overheard speaking to himself when they locked his bed-room door on him. To his promises there was no end. They took up all the columns in the local paper, and jostled out the advertisements. When a majority was declared in his favour Dumple was stunned, and took to throwing carrots through people's windows; and Crumple had to be comforted with hot tea and a jig, which the spinsters of the place danced round him hand in hand and howling. In the streets the eggs and dead cats made a night of it, and the hatters of the town got up a game of

football with all the head-dresses that fell off; but
Thumple meanwhile was being carried in triumph
to the Town Hall face downwards, and once there
and on his legs, he sang out, "Where's the wire
"box?" for he had heard of this intended gift, and
thought there was money in it.

He had not to wait long, for the Councillors
were all present, and in a minute the Mayor was
prodded forward, accompanied by the Man with the
Glass Eye. "I'm to pat you on the back," gasped
his worship, holding the box with both hands; and
at these words Thumple stooped gracefully, as if the
Council were going to play leap-frog with him. The
Mayor patted him with his fist, and all the sup-
porters of Dumple and Crumple did the same; then,
when Thumple had been picked up, the Mayor
added, "This is summut that'll prevent you from
"ever forgetting your friends at Swallowburgh," and
so saying, touched the spring and made the box fly
open.

But a great yell sprang from Thumple's throat,
for out of the wire box had leaped hundreds upon
hundreds of fleas, who flew into his hair, down his
neck, up his wristbands, and at that moment the
voice of the Man with the Glass Eye was heard
ejaculating,

"Burgess Thumple, each of those fleas is one of

"the promises you have made us. As fast as you
"discharge a promise one flea will leave you; but
"you will not be quit of them all till every one of
"your promises down to the smallest—represented
"by the littlest of these fleas—has been discharged."
"Take off those fleas!" raved Thumple, staggering
about under the stings, and rolling his head in a
window-curtain; but the Mayor and Councillors, the
Man with the Glass Eye, and a committee of shrieking sisters who had stumped for Crumple, parted in
two rows to right and left, and scampered out of
his presence. In another minute Thumple was seen
bounding down the High Street like an india-rubber
ball, and such was his pace that his heels seemed
to rap against the nape of his neck. The dead cats
and the hatters, the eggs and Dumple with his carrots, fled at sight of him, all panic-stricken; and he
vanished hooting into the night, did this maddened,
flea-bitten man.

No. 15.—The Valentine.

MR. FLIPP, who was everybody's friend but his own, sat directing envelopes one 13th of February in his study, and, when he had finished directing, he spent an hour passing his tongue over the backs of postage-stamps as he had seen other people do on like occasions. He had addressed valentines to all his kinsfolk and acquaintances, and to persons he admired—thus, one that cost twopence to the Archbishop of Canterbury, and a penny valentine to each of the Cabinet Ministers to prove his loyalty. But when he had exhausted his roll of friends and left none of the State dignitaries uncared for, he had still one valentine remaining. It represented a man in vermilion trousers being hanged by a man with jagged teeth, whilst a black-eyed woman stood in the background and rained tears into a pewter pot. The colour of this lady's eyes was not an effect of Nature, but of manual art—or science—and under the picture were printed some verses which seemed to give the pith of the whole story. Mr. Flipp, holding this valentine in one hand, twirled his pen with the other and sucked the inky nib of it, for he was lost in meditation. After some minutes he took up an envelope, and addressed his last valentine as folfows:—"*To the dirty little boy who sweeps the cross-*"*ing at the corner of Grig Street.*"

This dirty little boy was on his knees poring over a mud-pie of his making, when the postman cuffed him on the ears by way of a double-knock, and dropped the missive into his hands. Up to that day the dirty boy had never heard of valentines —nor deserved to hear of them, for the disorder of his mind surpassed the uncleanliness of his person; he did not know his catechism, and could tell nothing about Jonah and the whale. But an hour after the receipt of his valentine he might have been seen squatting under a lamp-post, with a face bedazed as if some high wind had come and swept part of his older self away; and from that hour the cats and dogs who passed along Grig Street marked him as an altered lad. It was not that he combed his hair or caused patches to be inserted in those portions of his garments where such amendments were needed; but he was self-absorbed and civil. He abstained from palming off his bad halfpence on to the apple-woman who sat near the pillar-box, as his prudent custom had been; and whenever he had time to spare, he drew his valentine from under his shirt and studied it with rapt attention. One day, emboldened by those sun's rays which are as a golden wine which Nature pours out to the wineless, the dirty boy gathered courage enough to stop a stout man waddling on his way to business, and to ask, "Wot's this?" pointing as he did so to the first line of print under his valentine. But the gracious Briton on his way to business gave him a kick which sent him into the roadway, and added, "Go and be hanged!" Now as the picture was one of a man being suspended by the neck, it seemed to the dirty boy that this "Go and be hanged!" must be just the correct interpretation; all that puzzled him was the kick, for there was nothing to show that the victim in vermilion trousers had been pedally propelled into the roadway before being strung up by the man with jagged teeth.

It took the dirty boy weeks and weeks to work out this problem, and other weeks and weeks before he learned that the piece of print he had pointed out was simply the letter Z, and that the kick into the roadway and the accompanying compliment were a mere facetious gloss of the business-like Briton's own. For all this, first impressions are tenacious as Whigs to Government posts, and the dirty boy's first impressions were that somebody had an earnest desire to see him hanged. He could read the print now, and understood that the man with vermilion trousers had come to his rope's end owing directly or indirectly to the pewter pot and that woman with the blackened eyes; and the inference he drew from this choking lesson was that the unknown sender of the valentine had divined, with a prophetic insight into the future, that he (the dirty boy) would come to a rope's end through the same agencies.

To spite this unknown sender, the dirty boy grimly resolved that this should never be. Pewter pots, black-eyed women, men with jagged teeth and vermilion trousers became objects of hourly abhorrence against which he prayed on bended knees, and against which he emphatically warned all the tenants of Grig Street by means of texts which he traced in the mud of the roadway with his broom.

It is a great thing to have a principle in life, and on his anti-pewter-black-eye-jagged-teeth-and-vermilion-trouser principles this dirty boy rose as high as game six weeks old, and higher. By never drinking his beer out of a pewter, but always out of a glass, he could see through the side whether the liquor was clear or thick, and thus be assured of having his money's worth, besides earning a reputa-

tion as a connoisseur in brewing. By eschewing
men with jagged teeth he avoided numerous undesirable acquaintances, for there is a subtle connexity
between teeth and digestion, digestion and temper,
temper and serviceability—things which are like four
clever rats holding one another by the tail. As to
women, he would hear of none who had not turquoise
eyes; and here, again, his principles steadfastly be-
friended him, for blue-eyed women suffer one to lead
a quiet life now and then, when they have their own
way. Let it be added that the dirty boy's rise was
as signally rapid as it was high. From sweeping
rubbish off the pavements he began to sweep money
into his pockets, and then he swept everything before him. He went into the City, engaged in trade,
was returned to the Common Council by his Ward,
and became reverentially noted from Cornhill to
Temple Bar as "the Alderman who would never
"wear vermilion trousers." Another thing that was
observed in him was this: whenever in the courteous
debates of business or municipal affairs anyone
said to him, "Go and be hanged!" he would
plant his fists on the table, and roar with an
energy that impressed all beholders, "No, that I
"won't!"

But, meanwhile, what had become of Mr. Flipp,
the primary cause of all this change? Had he loved

9*

himself more he might have kept step with the dirty little boy in the latter's march towards fame and turtle-soup. But, knowing the blemishes of his own character, and loathing them, he could never be brought to consider himself with common patience, and all things that might have tended to his personal comfort or aggrandisement he opposed from conscientious motives. Frequently could his friends be heard arguing with him at the top of their voices that he should care for his own interests, and spend his money on himself instead of on others; but he would mildly answer, "You don't know myself as I do," and saying this, would bite his nails as if glad to lessen some part at least of his uninteresting self. The consequence was that Mr. Flipp and the dirty little boy were like the two buckets in a well—as fast as one rose the other went down. Mr. Flipp went down out of men's dining-rooms, down out of their haunts, conversations, thoughts, and finally down out of their very knowledge — lower and lower every day he went, like Spanish securities, or like the American people looking for a Chief Justice.

There comes a time, however, when a man can go no lower—unless he takes a header into the abyss of Irish politics—and, therefore, one morning an elderly man might have been seen sweeping the crossing in Grig Street who had swept it every day for the past eleven months. He seemed stationary in the post which the dirty little boy had so efficiently filled in days gone by; but at odd moments he would pause in the midst of the crossing, address himself a severe rebuke as to his own unworthiness, and give himself a halfpenny, which he would drop into the pocket of the first underpaid policeman who passed that way. On the morning in question—which was a fresh February morning with a fog that made the sun look like a heavenly poached egg—the man had justly fined himself twopence because he had caught himself suspecting that the coffee he had taken at an early stall might not be pure Mocha, when, bobbing through the fog, there came upon him the postman, who held out an envelope with a twopenny stamp, and said, "Here's a walentine for you." It was in truth St. Valentine's Day, and glancing at the envelope, the crossing-sweeper could read on it this direction: *"To the dirty man who sweeps "the crossing at the corner of Grig Street."* He let fall his broom, which was instantly run over and broken by a coal-van full of blackened bricks to be charged as Wallsend, and, having fined himself all the money in his pockets for this wastefulness, he drew out the valentine and took a long, mindful look into the past.

For this crossing-sweeper was no other than Mr.

Flipp; and the man who had sent the valentine could be no one else than the dirty little boy who had been warned from pewter, dark-eyed women, and jagged teeth by the example of the man in vermilion trousers. Of this much Mr. Flipp felt persuaded; but his persuasion would have been of but little use to him had there not, by some hazard, slipped into the envelope the card of the sender: *"Mr. Alderman Flapp, Pudding Lane."* Armed with this card Mr. Flipp went to Guildhall, where he knew Mr. Alderman Flapp would be dispensing justice upside down from ten o'clock till dusk; and there he waited in a yard till justice had been administered—that is, little fines to citizens who had belaboured their wives, and long terms of imprisonment to others who had thrashed City merchants. When at last Mr. Alderman Flapp emerged, swathed in a comforter and in a flowing self-consciousness of equity, Mr. Flipp approached on the tips of his holeful boots, and whispered, "I am the dirty crossing-"man; are you the dirty crossing-boy?"—and in another moment they were locked in each others' arms. "I owe everything to you," sobbed the worthy Alderman, rocking to and fro in his tenderness; "my wife "who has blue eyes, my footmen who have all "straight teeth, and my wardrobe in which you would "not find one blessed pair of vermilion trousers; and

"all these things are at your disposal!" Fervidly
and frantically they kissed each other under the
lamp-post, again in Fleet Street, and once again opposite the Mansion House, where they stopped for
the purpose, interrupting the traffic. But this City
idyll is one too beautiful to be deflowered by further
description. It got known at the Bank, in Lothbury,
up Capel Court, and down Pudding Lane that Alderman Flapp had found a second father, and that if
he had possessed a daughter he would have given
her to him in marriage. But as he had no daughter
he gave him five shillings instead and made him
happy.

No. 16.—The Banquet in Downing Street.

IN one of those hours of depression when one feels doubtful as to whether one shall take dinner or a meat-tea, I took nothing but my hat, and found myself in Downing Street. No well-known forms of clerks or messengers brushed by me, the sentries had got into their boxes because of the fog, and I should have walked alone in the street if it had not been for a spare man in evening dress who came noiselessly behind me with india-rubber goloshes, then passed, and would have disappeared in the gloom had he not dropped a pair of white cotton gloves, which I picked up. They were gloves such as waiters wear, and I ran to restore them to their owner, who proved to be well stricken in years—just the man to have interested an undertaker. He thanked me for the gloves and would have proceeded on his quickened way; but I had been impressively struck by some words of his about certain other servants in beautiful clothes whom he should have been ashamed to meet bare-handed; so I inquired of him whether there was an official dinner in the street that night. The old man stared and answered with bated breath, drawing closer to me for the purpose, "Why, don't you know, Sir—"but in course you can't know—to-night is THE "DINNER!" and, whispering this, he looked round to see whether policeman, sentry, or area cat had overheard him.

I knew nothing of THE DINNER further than that nobody had invited me to it, and this much I confessed in a tone of gloom; whereat the old man exclaimed, with not one but many shakes of his ancient head, "I have waited at a dozen of 'em, Sir, "and my fathers and forbears waited at 'em too, "ever since our family began; but it may be years "before there's another, and I shall likely be dead "then, so I should have been sorry if they'd a seen "me without the gloves."

This he said with an emphasis so deep that the sense of his indebtedness to me was evidently uppermost in his aged mind, and he twice fingered the brim of his hat to me as he prepared to rush on into the fog, declaring that his moments were precious. But he had not explained to me the nature of THAT DINNER which had seemed to fill his mouth—he had not said who were the diners nor what the bill of fare—and I was curiously moved to catechise him on these points before his india-rubber goloshes bore him out of my sight. At my first words, however, he turned round in a supplicating manner, holding up a silver watch to the gaslight and exclaimed, "I wouldn't be late, Sir, for the other "servants would shame me; but you picked up "my gloves, and perhaps you'd like to see THE "DINNER?" He had got ahead of me now, his voice came through the fog as if he had melted away, and with him THE DINNER appeared to melt too out of my reach, making me run forward in a state of panic I had never experienced before to overtake it.

"Yes, I should like to sit down at the dinner," was my panting answer.

"Ah, but you can't sit down at it, Sir," quavered the voice feebly out of the fog; "you can help me "hand the dishes round, and you'll never forget the "sight, not if you live as old as the crows." This was a strange communication, but I faltered a consent, not knowing why I should hand dishes round when so many of the population would have been glad to have me at a meat-tea. Yet impelled forward by the desire to see something more of that mystic waiter with the goloshes, I caught him up, and he stammered to me to follow him. The clock in the Victoria Tower was chiming out rhythmically just then the three- quarters past seven o'clock, and we disappeared together into the official residence of the Premier, he first, and I at his heels.

The whole house was wrapped in silence and obscurity. There were no lights in the windows, no sounds of treading in the passages, no voices in the offices, and above all no preparations of any sort for dinner or for so much as a glass of sherry with a few biscuits round it. The venerable waiter had entered the house with a key of his own, and in the vestibule he lit a coil-taper, which, as we passed down corridors, threw a pale blue light on the chambers where clerks and junior lords sit and snub the taxpayer in the morning.

At last we reached a door, outside which the waiter paused, put a finger on his lips, and began removing his goloshes, hat, and overcoat, all of which he laid on the mat, motioning me to do the same with my own open-air garments. Then he drew on his cotton gloves, knocked gently at the door, and received from a voice whose tones were well known to me the answer to come in.

"Is it you, Ganymede?" asked the earnest voice, which proceeded from a chair near the chim-

ney, in which the dying embers of a fire were
smouldering.

"Yes, Sir," replied the waiter, with the same
hushed respect as if he had been in a sick room;
and to me he added, under his breath, "My name
"ain't Ganymede—it's William—but the gentleman
"loves his joke, bless his heart!"

"Well, this evening has come at last, Ganymede,"
proceeded the voice, in tones quite exempt from
jocularity; "but who is that behind you?" and the
crouching form whence the voice issued gave a start
in its arm-chair.

"No one to speak of, Sir—no one but a friend,"
protested the aged William; "he's come to help me
"wait, for I'm an old man, Sir, and this may be the
"last of these dinners I shall ever wait at."

"Well, well, tell me when the dinner is ready,"
rejoined the voice, lugubriously; and William and I
crossed the room to an opposite door, where my
companion said, "There's no call for you to come
"in with me, Sir. You can stay here while I help
"dish up the dinner, then when it's ready you'll go
"about with me and pour out the wines." I nodded,
and remained in the room where the crouching form
was. I stood unperceived behind his chair, and
HE, thinking himself alone, threw broken-winged

words into the fire-place, such as Homer might have uttered when the spleenful fits were on him.

"Five years—five years!" he muttered; and if I had not recognised him at first sight, I should have known then that this was the GREAT LIGHT who during five years had governed England—THE LIGHT whose lustre was now fading away like those dying embers in the fire. Often he stretched out his fingers over the grate as if to catch a last remnant of the warmth; and meanwhile a muffled clatter of dishes and a dull hum of voices became audible in the adjoining room.

Full half-an-hour we remained together, He sitting and murmuring to himself, I standing motionless and mute. And then by degrees the noise in the next chamber grew louder and louder, till abruptly a pair of folding-doors were thrown back, a torrent of light streamed into the room, and William appeared on the threshold with a napkin over his arm, announcing "Dinner is on the table, "Sir."

Then I looked and saw a large banqueting-hall laid out for countless guests, who seemed to start out from the wainscoats or come out from the frames of pictures, and most of whom were clad richly in the garbs of past ages. A great shout arose among them, half curiosity, half mirth, as the whilom

GREAT but now WANING LIGHT made his way to the seat at the head of the central table; and it flashed upon me in this moment that here was THE DINNER at which Premiers who are on the eve of leaving office are allowed to meet their predecessors. They were British Premiers I had before me, all come back from the night of time to hear the WANING LIGHT make his valedictory speech and to pronounce their own ghostly verdicts upon it.

Ah! how well the statesmen faces stood out recognisable and familiar from old prints or historic portraits! Wolsey in his flowing scarlet, Cecil with hoary head, the stately Godolphin, witty Bolingbroke, keen Harley, Chatham with the wan and pallid face, jovial and plump Robert Walpole, Pitt with clear eyes and sharp nose upturned, fat Fox, little Perceval, prim Canning, and numberless others, down to portly Peel and urbane English Palmerston.

Proud and vibrating were the voices of these resusciated patriots as they recounted by what great deeds they had ennobled England, making her empire stretch from sea to sea, and her name fly from pinnacle to pinnacle, over higher and higher like an eagle on the wing. Glowing names of victories won and tyrannous nations humbled fell from their elated lips, and the more joyous spirits among them called upon the servants who surrounded them—William's predecessors in menial clothing of bygone years—to fill their glasses that they might hob-nob to the perpetual freedom and glory of Britain!

And all this while the WANING LIGHT sat mournfully eating his soup, the central figure of the horse-shoe table and the butt of all eyes. He was abashed, and more than once whispered to me in his low, earnest voice for sauterne, champagne, and other liquids, till I much feared these beverages would get into his thoughtful head and make him talk as if he were at Blackheath. He was not like Walpole, who emptied three bottles between the fish and the truffled Turkey; nor like Pitt, who pshawed French wines aside as only fit for women. But he had a comforting belief in his superiority over his fellow-guests—this I could see; and when their talk grew noisy and seemed to blare like trumpets in triumph he drew a *Daily Telegraph* from his coat-tails, and read therein the patents of immortality which the House of Levi had signed him.

By the end of the banquet his self-possession left me no apprehension whatever that he would break down in his speech from over-modesty. He seemed rather to fidget for the moment when he might rise to his legs and speak words that might

convert these reproachable Premiers of the past for
their excessive prodigalities with the public monies;
and when at last the lull of the toast period arrived,
his earnest features glowed like the brazen counter-
slab of a prosperous tradesman.

"Silence!" quavered William, bringing down an
ivory hammer on the table at the chairman's right,
and the assembly rose like one man, with features
aflame, glasses charged, and hands outstretched to
drink the toast which had been cried in that hall
from time out of mind—"*Old England, and con-
"found her enemies!*" But just as these words were
starting from William's shrunken lips the WANING
LIGHT put up his hand and covered this aged
toastmaster's lips.

"Let us confound nobody," he said, with pious
firmness; "and let us not drink to the sanguinary
"triumphs of field and flood, but to the peaceful
"victories of the Pound Sterling. My lords and
"gentlemen, I drink to Economy, and may the Em-
"pire of England grow less year by year in order
"that her responsibilities and expenses may be
"diminished! My lords and gentlemen, I drink to
"Arbitration, and may all kingdoms learn that this
"Liberal State will never go to war so long as she
"has a surplus to dispose of!"

He could add no more, for the diners were roaring with one voice, Chatham was clenching his fist, Pitt and Walpole flung bottles at him, till I was obliged to carry the WANING LIGHT out into the streets in my arms, and there I extinguished him with William's hat.

————

No. 17.—The Manx Cat.

THE more one sees of men the more one loves Manx cats of the tailless sort. This was the sentiment of Jenny Sweete, who sold French confectionery at a shop in the Burlington Arcade, and wished to be loved, as her highest quality chocolate did, for her own sake. Her Manx cat, whose name was Ephraim, approved this view, and he would frequently point out, with the sagacity peculiar to his race, that the majority of men who came into the Arcade to court Jenny were individuals of a frivolous turn, whose promises were friable. This he did by scratching them. One day he scratched a man in the Guards, who kicked him through the door, tail first—at least the tail would have gone first if Ephraim had possessed one; as it was, the last seen of him was his whiskers crashing through the glass front of a haircutter's opposite. Then the man in the Guards begged pardon, and said it was a mistake; there is no necessity for adding that he took the opportunity of kissing Jenny to prove how sincere were his feelings.

"Ah, you call it a mistake!" cried Jenny, indignantly disengaging herself, and rushing across the Arcade for her cat, who at this juncture reappeared in the custody of three haircutters. "I call "it base and wicked," sobbed she, returning with the haircutters and fondling the cat, who spat and squalled so that he could be heard up Savile Row.

There was a scene, full of music, and during its progress a crowd congregated outside, whilst Jenny continued, in vibrating tones, "You shall pay for all "that broken glass, and learn to love this cat like "your better self, so I tell you."

"I will pay for the broken glass," replied the Guardsman, with singular firmness, "but I will never "love that cat." Saying which he counted out some sovereigns to the haircutters, Jenny adding a pound of vanilla caramels for the youngest haircutter's child, who was cutting his grinder teeth.

"I repeat you *shall* love the cat," said Jenny, in great agitation, when the haircutters had vanished; "for look and see what's written above that table "where the oyster-patties stand!" And the Guardsman, glancing above the patties, saw, printed in gold letters on a purple ground, "LOVE ME LOVE MY "CAT."

"I shouldn't have believed it, 'pon my word," he remarked, dropping his eye-glass the better to see.

"Because you don't believe anything," retorted Jenny, with fire; "but you said you loved me, so you "shall grow to love the cat with a deep, tender, and "abiding love; and until you do he shall follow you "everywhere, and never leave you." This threat was too much to be endured, so the Guardsman planted his hat over his brow with a gesture of energy, and fled towards Bond Street. But the cat, obeying a stamp of Jenny's foot, bolted after him.

This Guardsman was quartered at Windsor; and Sheep Street, if we remember correctly, is the name of the thoroughfare where his barracks stood. At any rate you take the first right turning after passing the Town Hall, skirt Bachelor's Acre, and when you have reached a door with a bearskin and a sentry under it you march straight into the block of buildings to the left, and make yourself at home with the sherry and the hams unless the messman turns you out.

Now, leaving Paddington for Windsor the Guardsman was accompanied by the cat, who sat on the roof of the carriage and miawled at Ealing, Hanwell, the Slough porter, and all the other places and persons of interest down the line. Going up Thames Street, Windsor, the Guardsman struck five times at

the cat with his umbrella, kicked at him, pitched a
Bradshaw at his head, but all to no purpose. And
when he reached the barracks he shrieked, "Guard,
"turn out, and hunt that beast of a cat who has fol-
"lowed me from London!"

The guard turned out to a man, sergeant, bugler
and all, but "divil a bit," as the sentry expressed
it, could they catch that tailless cat, who careered
over the barrack-yard in leaps and bounds like Mr.
Gladstone's notion of Progress. The corporal took
a broom; the soldiers flung mess-tins and blacking-
brushes; the bugler threw a lantern with his might
and main, and hit the sergeant on the waist, making
him double up and drip with oil like a salad; and
the while the soldiers in the barrack-rooms started
from their beds, and threw up the sashes; the officers hurried to the windows in their night-gowns;
and the colonel was heard roaring from the landing,
"What's the row down there? Captain Dudd, are
"you sober?" Dudd was the Guardsman's name,
and he was perfectly sober, but the cat's doings had
made his nerves thrill like the strings of a fiddle,
and when, having been got between sheets by-and-
by, and hoping for rest, he saw the cat tumble down
the chimney on to his hearth-rug, no human power
could prevent him from jumping up and firing six
barrels of a revolver, with twice that number of

curses. He smashed his toilet glass, his sitz bath was riddled through and flooded the room with water, his dress-boots had holes shot through them, and two of the bullets brought down three pounds of the ceiling plaster; but Dudd might as well have blown six bread pellets out of a toothpick for all the cat cared.

Let it be stated at once that things could not be allowed to pass off in this way. When Dudd, in jaded plight, came down to parade in the morning, and sang out to his company, "Number one!" the sergeant who should have answered, "All present, "sir," was interrupted by the tailless cat, who jumped on to his shoulders, and squalled the reply in his stead. When the colonel, beside himself at this liberty, bellowed, "Catch that cat!" the brute took a header among the band's kettledrums, entangled himself between the drum-major's legs, and seemed to melt away into the gravel; but when the companies had formed fours for a march-out up the Long Walk, who should appear at the very head of the first company but this tailless cat again, who stood on his hind legs marking time just out of the reach of Dudd's foot and sword.

Hereon the colonel's wrath burst up like a magazine, and he holloaed out, with fury enough to loosen all the teeth in his head, "Companies! Halt!

"Dismiss! And five pounds to the man who kills "that cat!" The words were such as would have rent any other animal limb from limb, but this cat lost not so much as a hair of his fur by them. He evaded his pursuers; got into the mess-room, and kicked down the clock; a tray of soda-water and herrings going up to Captain Budd was strewn by him to the earth; sticks and stones hurled in search or his skull found out the skulls of other people, broke heads, and damaged furniture. Never since Inkermann had a battalion of Guards gone to work in such style, but never were results so pitiful. The colonel, who quivered on his horse like a watch-spring, galloped about the yard till the perspiration soaked him through, and at last, reining in beside miserable Dudd, he shook his fist, and yelled, "What the devil do you mean by bringing that cat "here, Dudd? If you don't get rid of him I'll write "to the Horse Guards! I'll force you to sell out, by "heavens! I'll court-martial you!"

"But it isn't my cat," whimpered Dudd, whose boots were covered with soil, and whose sword had snapped off short at the hilt from striking a door-scraper behind which Ephraim had dodged.

"Don't explain to me, sir!" howled the colonel, at whom the tailless cat was just then making faces from the roof of the guard-room. "You and that

"cat are in league, by gad! Get rid of him in
"four-and-twenty hours, or I'll know the reason."

So an hour after this, wretched Dudd might have
been seen steaming towards London again, with the
object of calling on Jenny and appealing to her feelings; and, as before, the cat sat on the carriage top,
despite remonstrances and missiles from the guard.
This time he miawled at Langley, Uxbridge, and
West Drayton—places of interest which he had forgotten to salute on the night previous.

Need it be said to those who know woman's
conciliatory proclivities that Jenny absolutely declined to relieve Dudd of the tailless cat's company?
"It's written over the oyster-patties, '*Love me love
"my cat*,'" she answered, with great spirit and de-
cision.

"But I do love the cat," groaned downcast Dudd,
hoping by this fiction to escape the responsibilities
of his dilemma. But Jenny saw through the un-
manly device, and exposed it.

"If you loved the cat," said she, scornfully, "he
"would come when you called him, jump on your
"knee, and eat fish-bones out of your hand."

"Pooty puss, pooty puss!" whistled poor Dudd,
stooping forward and rubbing the fore-finger and
thumb of his left dog-skin glove together; for it was
occurring to him that if only the cat would come on

his knee he might strangle him for his pains or drown him in a bowl of stewed pears that stood on the counter. But the cat kept a cautious distance, and sat under a row of raised pies, closing one eye at Dudd and licking his paws with great deliberation one after another, so that Jenny exclaimed, "You see he will have nothing to say to you, "though at ordinary times he is a most lovable "cat."

"D——n the cat!" ejaculated Dudd, with intense feeling, as he fled from the shop again and strode down the Arcade towards Piccadilly. He had a clear purpose: he would go to Scotland Yard and bring that tailless cat under the notice of the police.

But he had not got half-way down St. James's Street, followed persistently by Ephraim at ten yards' distance, when he became aware of someone dogging his footsteps, and, turning round,. he was confronted by a small, affable man, who said, "I beg "pardon, but I notice you are attended by a black "cat with white stockings. May I ask whether he is "yours? He is a Manx cat."

"The brute has got no tail, if that's what you "mean," answered Dudd, savagely. "If you kill him "for me any time before to-night you shall have a "hundred pounds, 'pon my soul."

"Kill him?—no, I think not!" rejoined the affable man, with surprise.

"One more question: is the cat's name Ephraim?"

"Yes," answered Dudd, looking moody horrors at the cat, who was surveying him coolly from the cab-stand, "yes, I believe the beast has some un-"christian name of that sort."   .

"Then my name is Quilles, and I am a lawyer," replied the affable man, with elation: "and allow "me to congratulate you, for that tailless cat has just "inherited twenty-five thousand pounds a-year and "at least three of the Windward Islands."

"You don't say it?" exclaimed Dudd, dropping his umbrella with astonishment.

"Yes, I do," answered Quilles, "and you'll easily "understand it. Lady Tabitha, a rich client of mine "living at Beaumaris, had a she-cat, who was mar-"ried with her full consent to a tom-cat from the "Isle of Man, who held an important post in the "House of Keys—in fact he looked after the mice "there. From this happy union were born seven "tailless kittens, of whom six found an early death "in a bucket, but the seventh survived to be a com-"fort to his mother, and was named Ephraim. He "disappeared mysteriously however one night some "years ago, and was advertised for in the *Times* in "the usual way, but to no purpose. In the mean-

"time his parents both died, and Lady Tabitha,
"who dwindled rapidly towards her grave after their
"loss, made a will bequeathing her whole estate to
"this lost Ephraim, if so be that he could be
"found; a codicil explaining that Ephraim's money
"should be enjoyed during his lifetime, and devolve
"at his death either on his owner or on the person
"he loved best, according as I in my discretion as
"arbitrator should decide."

"You are quite sure of all this—that is, you've
"not been lunching?" inquired dazzled Dudd, with
fixed attention.

"I am quite sure, and I'll take a glass of hock
"with you with pleasure since you're so pressing,"
answered affable Quilles.

"Then the money'll be mine," asserted Dudd,
thoughtfully. "You see that cat is desperately fond
"of me; he won't leave me five minutes."

That night a doctor's certificate despatched to
Windsor obtained Dudd a month's leave on the
score of ill-health, and next day the Guardsman
hired a villa at Richmond and laid himself out to
make things pleasant for the cat. Muffins and
cream were the things provided for Ephraim's daily
breakfast; cutlets and turbot formed the staple of
his luncheon; in the evening he made himself unwell with as much game and whitebait as he could

manage. That his nights might be smooth, Dudd bought him a Turkey rug; and that his health might never suffer from want of fresh air Dudd hired an outrigger and sculled up from Richmond to Kingston Lock every morning, with Ephraim squatting behind the stretcher.

Such treatment breeds a community of views between animate beings, and the tailless cat relaxed his suspiciousness so far as to leave off spitting when Dudd made affectionate advances towards him. Still he was wary of letting himself be touched, and would on no account come when called; but this, according to Dudd, was a remnant of shyness engendered by that ill-timed kick through the haircutter's window, and when the shyness had worn off Dudd hoped to stand in this position; either the love borne him by the cat would qualify him to sue for Jenny's hand, the £25,000 a-year, and the three Windward Isles, or if Jenny refused her hand he would go to law with her and prove that the cat's love for him surpassed all other loves, and by such means he would obtain the pounds and the islands without Jenny. Pending this consummation he contrived that Jenny should know nothing of Ephraim's heritage, and he waited patiently in the villa at Richmond until Mr. Quilles, who thought him owner of the cat, should write to him that the first quarter of

Ephraim's income was ready for drawing at the banker's.

But Dudd had apparently but small experience of inheritance, for before the tailless cat could be put in possession of his dues a few formalities had to be gone through. In the first place some collaterals of Lady Tabitha disputed her will, alleging that the property was to be divided equally among all the issue of her ladyship's cat married to the Manx tom from the House of Keys, and they produced a tailless cat of their own, said to be Ephraim's eldest brother, happily rescued from drowning in the bucket. This cause came on for hearing before Sir James Hannen, and was luminously argued during twenty-six of the Dog-days. The first Windward Island went away in costs. Sir James took time to consider his judgment, then pronounced that all Ephraim's tailless brothers would be co-heirs, and ordered fifteen of the witnesses on either side to be indicted for perjury. The next round was fought out in the Court of Chancery by means of affidavits, injunctions, interpleaders, files of questions, and demurrers. The costs of this stage swallowed up the second Windward Isle and part of the third, for not only did the five other tailless kittens supposed to have been drowned in the bucket reappear as full-grown claimants to co-heirship, but ninety-three other tailless cats uprose with backers to affirm that they were the offspring of Ephraim's mother by divers marriages unavowed.

One regrets to state that many painful things were sworn to about Ephraim's parents during these hearings at Lincoln's Inn. His mother's chastity was impugned by the Law Officers of the Crown, and his father's relations with the mice in the House of Keys were subjected to severe comments from the Bench. But all went well in the end, for when the Vice-Chancellor had given his judgment, the Lord Chancellor in the Court above quashed it, after which the Judicial Committee of the Privy Council quashed what both Courts had ruled, then what Sir James Hannen had decided, and finally ordered everybody to start afresh as if nothing had happened. This brought all the parties into the Common Pleas, where Ephraim stood as sole heir defending his inheritance against two hundred and ninety-seven new tailless cats who had started up, each purporting to be the only true Ephraim; and at this point the editors of the *Times, Pall Mall Gazette,* and the *Morning Post* were sent to Newgate for printing that 296 of the lot must be impostors, which was treated as contempt of court. It is a pleasure to record, however, that here again Ephraim triumphed, at no greater expense than the second half of the

third Windward Isle and the first half of the remaining income; and after this nothing was left for
his counsel but to clear up these three points:—
1. Was the cat Ephraim tailless-born, or had he
ridden himself of his tail for the purposes of the
cause? 2. Was the fur on his back his own or some
other cat's? 3. Had he grown since he was a kitten,
and, if so, why? This case being only one of iden-
tity, took no more than three hundred sittings to dispose of, and when it was ended Ephraim was gra-
ciously allowed to have his rest.

It was a glad day for Captain Dudd when he
was apprised at Richmond that the tribunals of this
mighty kingdom had absorbed every halfpenny of
the tailless cat's inheritance, and had left him, besides, thirteen and fourpence indebted to Mr. Quilles,
but for all this had rendered him justice, and put
him in calm possession of his rights. As if to mark
his own gratification at this strange fact, the tailless
cat for the first time in his life leaped up that day
on to his friend Dudd's knee, and accepted from
him so many fish-bones that he choked. When
Dudd returned to the Burlington Arcade a week
afterwards he carried a paper parcel under his arm,
and inside it Ephraim stuffed and with glass eyes.

But consolation was at hand. It was years and
years since he had last seen Jenny, for what between

Westminster Hall and Lincoln's Inn the minutes slip away somehow. Dudd's month's leave was expired, too, and he had forgotten to renew it, so that he had no social status in particular, except that paper parcel with stuffed Ephraim in it. But Jenny had some oyster-patties fresh baked which she made him eat with a spoon, and a proposal which she poured out with a glass of Madeira. Said she, when Dudd had told his story for the third time—and all of it was new to her, for she read nothing in the papers but the births and marriages—said she, with a smile, "Your love for that cat proves you can be trusted to "love me, so we'll keep this shop together; but in "the daytime you'll want exercise, you know, so "to-morrow you'll be gazetted to one of the beadle-"ships of the Arcade." And honest Jenny was true to her generous word. Dudd is now one of those two beadles who mount guard over Arcadia to keep its groves chaste and clean.

No. 18.—The Third-Floor Lodger.

THE housemaid, having put the kettle on the kitchen fire to boil, tidied her hair opposite a corner of broken looking-glass, and then ran out to the police-station to give information about the mysterious disappearance of the third-floor lodger. This was in a street well known to all those who resided in it, and the house whence the lodger had mysteriously disappeared was numbered "9" on the door and "65" in the Directory, to prevent confusion. It will be well to remember that the man had passed by the name of Toity, which was as good a name as any other for the use he made of it, and the mystery of his disappearance consisted not so much in the absence itself—for he was a man who often forgot himself, and might well have done so on this occasion, rambling obliviously through the town—as in an envelope which he left in his shaving-dish addressed to his landlady, and with a prayer that it should not be opened until three days after his mysterious disappearance had been noticed.

Obediently to these instructions the missive was of course unsealed before the disappearance had been noticed a quarter of an hour, and three painful statements were then brought to light: first, that Mr. Toity had been worried in mind and body by the Cock who crowed in the yard of No. 10; second, that he always disliked that Cock; last and least, that he had been concerned in some murders. These items were unfolded to the Inspector at the station whilst the latter sat in his dock eating a bloater on a slice of bread-and-butter, for it was breakfast-time. When he had munched the bread-and-butter, and wrapped the fishbone in a slip of paper to use as a comb should combs ever grow expensive, he looked at the housemaid, and said, with conviction, "You should have washed your face, "Mary, before coming with news so serious as this "'ere.' "My name ain't Mary," answered the damsel, pertly; "and as to washin' my face I'd like to see "you up to your ears in blacking, doing boots for "the Second-pair-back." "There's a Second-pair-"back then?" asked the Inspector, as he stirred his coffee with his forefinger, being regardless of con-gruities when his zeal for the public good was aroused. "Yes, you may bet five pounds on it," answered the housemaid, standing on one leg, her name being Hopper. "Then we'll arrest "him on suspicion," said the Inspector, thoughtfully.

So they arrested the Second-pair-back. He was a struggling man, who had applied himself to learn whether wood-shavings could ever be employed as a substitute for hay in stuffing horse-hair sofas; and his drawers were full of sawdust, which he intended fabricating into cough lozenges. When they put handcuffs on him he protested, but was warned that whatever he said might be used against him; and by-and-by when he sought to defend himself in face of the magistrate his worship repeated this warning, and had him hurried back to the cells before he could speak.

Meanwhile, the police, having explored Mr. Toity's rooms for proofs of their suspicions, made a careful entry of six paper collars, one toothbrush, half-a-pint of hair-dye, and an ace of clubs marked with the name of the Second-pair-back and the figures 3s. 6d., all of which sufficed to justify a remand, for it became patent to the meanest intellect that the Second-pair-back, being indebted 3s. 6d. to Mr. Toity, had first murdered him with a bludgeon, and then concealed his body somewhere under sawdust. These facts were borne out by the testimony of three experts in handwriting. All three being shown the letter addressed in Mr. Toity's name to the landlady

unanimously took oath that it had been written by
the Two-pair-back, until evidence was brought that
this backward man could not write at all; whereon
the experts retreated in good order, but swore the
letters corresponded with two others found in the
Two-pair-back's room—the one being a prescription
from a chemist in Soho, the other a note announcing
marmalade from a maiden aunt in Dundee. At this
juncture an incident came athwart everybody, for
an epistle was posted by Mr. Toity himself begging
that all proceedings might be stayed against the
Two-pair-back, for that he (Toity) was alive and unwell. This of course failed to shake the experts,
who each went their ways and wrote magazine articles to prove that the whole affair had been mis-
managed. The Two-pair-back did not read the
articles, for after a fortnight had been spent in considering whether Mr. Toity's letter was admissible as
evidence, he was liberated, and his time was then
chiefly spent in wondering how he should pay a soli-
citor who had undertaken to make a speech for him,
and who now made him a speech about his fees.

But one detective, who was pained to think that
nobody was going to be hanged through this affair,
began from this day to set a watch on the Cock
who crowed at No. 10. After all, Mr. Toity had
confessed to committing murder, and he had men-

tioned the Cock in terms of aversion, nothing was
more probable than that he and that bird had plan-
ned their misdeeds in company, and now hated
each other as accomplices in crime are prone to do.
The detective who arrived at this conclusion was not
a novice in the science of deducing. When a policeman he had struck for more pay; and having also
one night struck an old gentleman on the ears he
had shaved off his beard on the morrow so that
somebody else might be identified in the matter.
Owing to these and other exploits, which proved an
inherent capacity for inferring where his own interest
lay, the man had risen to much honour in the force,
so that he had been promoted to detect offenders
as above said, and now he meant to detect that
Cock.

With a posy of smiles on his lips he hovered
round the housemaid at No. 10, who was best friend
to Miss Hopper at No. 9, and who went across the
road every day at twelve to fetch the beer. He
blandished this maiden about her cap-strings, about
the musical clip-clap of her shoes trudging over the
macadam, and about the playful waywardness of her
eyes, one of which would beam upon him as he
spoke whilst the other obliquely scanned the far
horizon visible at the extreme end of the thoroughfare. Nor were these small coins of amiability thrown

away. It was but a little while before the Detective was initiated into all the habits of the Cock, by many odds the most dissipated fowl in the neighbourhood. He was told of his goings on in the small hours, of his flippancy and strutting ways, and at length he was admitted to see him one morning after a periwinkle breakfast garnished with water-cress. The feast was spread in the kitchen, and the kitchen was on a level with the yard. It was between his third cup of tea and his fourth that, leaning over the window-sill, the Detective took a deep, searching, and scrutinous look at the Cock, who was lording it over the flags with his seven wives—feeble, foolish, and cackling poultry. But now a stirring thing occurred; for whilst the Detective was immersed in his contemplation with the housemaid, the cook and the page standing behind to sing chorus to whatever criticisms he might please to offer, the Cock perceived the group, reared his crest, strode forward, and without more preface uttered a *cock-a-doodle-do-o-o* so shrill, long, and defiant that the Detective started back as if he had needles in his ears. It was particularly the final notes of the *doo-o-o-o* that showed the animus of the fowl, for he had raised them to such a pitch that his silly wives became dazed, and flustered about in a panic, screaming *cluck-cluck-cluck-cluck-a-deedle.* The Detective, with a startled look, put up both hands to hush whatever the cook and housemaid might have to say, and then the Cock, making another stride forward, launched a new crow more piercing than the first, then a third, then a fourth, and so on to hoarseness, pausing an instant between each crow to jerk his head on one side and brace himself for the next effort. At. first the Detective stood his ground manfully; then he receded a step. Towards the fifth crow he receded two steps at a time, and when he could recede no longer by reason of the plaster wall he took to his heels, and when he had taken to his heels he took to swearing, and by-and-by he might have been seen taking to drink to drive the deafening memory of that cock away. "Now, drat the bird," cried the cook, in wrath, as she flung a whole plateful of toast crusts at the now silent chanticleer; "he's just bin and spoiled "Mr. Hoighty's breakfast."

But the Cock at No. 10 had done more than. spoil Mr. Hoighty's breakfast. Just as you and I after a spell of "Lohengrin" or the "Tannhäuser" go home to our nightmares with a wild notion of the power of sound, so the Detective, pondering over what the Cock had said, felt as if a number of other cocks had got into his head, and were splitting wood there with bill-hooks. It was a unique feeling. The crashing of cabs and 'buses against each other, the vans running over cripples and children, the groans of elderly men slipping down over orange-peel, the yelping of mad dogs—all the familiar melodies of a well-ordered metropolitan street had never preyed upon him to this extent, and every day of the next week he returned as though fascinated to the spot where the Cock had crowed, and listened to him again. But he did not go through the kitchen. He had found a wall which overlooked the yard, and whence, by standing on a tub and resting his chin on the broken glass that adorned the ridge, he could see the Cock, who, descrying him, would wink, then open his beak and crow lustily, as if here was a man whose education had to be taken up from the beginning, but who should lose nothing from having tarried unduly. Was it that Mr. Hoighty proved a more apt pupil than Mr. Toity? Anyhow it was not ten days before he, too, mysteriously disappeared, leaving a nine days' wonder behind him; but never a line of explanation.

He had no need to explain. Strong in the gifts with which the wisdom of the Cock had endowed him, he went forth to new destinies, looking the Future briskly in the face like an enemy that is to be wrestled with and conquered. For what was the moral conveyed by that boastful fowl's ascendancy over seven shrivelled hens if not this, that a loud speech and hearty makes a fine-feathered bird? From such premises to the belief in crowing as a profession the gulf is narrow, and Mr. Hoighty, who had pined all his life after fine feathers, cleared it at a bound. He began to be seen in the parks haranguing the multitude. He belonged to associations for putting down everything that stood in his way, promoting popular diseases, releasing criminals, setting every man loose upon the man next him, with the Devil let free into the bargain to keep order among them all. Of the principles that minister to the comfort of modern peoples—the supremacy of the ignorant and greedy, the all-blessedness of combining to howl, the contempt for one's grandfather —he was a valuable exponent, and his voice would spin loudly through the trees like the music of an Irish harp as he glossed on these favourite themes.

But one day as he stood out there in one of those parks, with his right arm encircling the trunk of an oak and his left sawing the breath of the few thousand progressists who had been convened to hear him talk, he saw a man who neither applauded nor wept, but sat simply on the grass eating an orange and dropping walnut-shells into his hat most musingly. Nothing disturbed the equanimity of this man; so when Mr. Hoighty had fallen with fatigue and fulness from his oak, like an acorn well ripe, he approached the orange-eater and said, "Principles "don't appear to trouble you much, my friend."

"No, there's nothing to be had by 'em," answered the man, sadly, as he stowed the last piece of orange into his mouth.

"Heigh, but you're wrong there: everything's to "be had by 'em if you only wait long enough for "the crop," was Mr. Hoighty's thankful answer.

"I don't think it," replied the stranger, stroking his ears absently with the orange-peel and looking to see that all his walnut-shells were safe; "I tried "'em without profit, and now these shells and this "bit of peel are all the money I have, which comes "of listening to that Cock."

"The Cock!" echoed Mr. Hoighty, starting back; and there was a moment's fateful silence, during which the thousands of progressists packed in rows like haddocks held their breaths. "Then you're Mr. "Toity?" gasped the ex-Detective, laying hold of the long-lost third-floor lodger's neck and dragging him to his heels. "Come with me. You committed "murder."

"Yes, it's a fact," choked the recovered Mr. Toity; "but you're an accessory after the fact, so "we'll be tried together. I murdered Truth, Good-"sense, and, I am sorry to say, the Queen's English "every day of my life after I had seen that Cock."

Saying which he made a clutch at his walnut-shells and got the orange-peel between his teeth. But Mr. Hoighty released him with a shove. "If that's all, "we're neither of us guilty, for those things you "speak of are still alive. They take a deal of kill-"ing."

And it seems they do.

———

No. 19.—The Sky-Blue Dress.

IF you, who do me the honour to read this, are a lady, you will understand, dear Madam, what emotion can be inspired by the sight of a sky-blue dress of Lyons silk trimmed with Brussels lace, and looped up with little bunches of white rosebuds and forget-me-nots. This satisfactory garment was exposed to the public admiration in the window of a fashionable firm of silk-mercers, and the admiring public consisted on a certain midday occasion of a butcher-boy carrying one pound of veal cutlets in his tray, and of a pretty girl some seventeen springs old with a basket of collarettes and cuffs on her arm. The butcher-boy soon had enough of the dress and went off, he and his cutlets; but the girl shifted her position slowly, now to the right, now to the left, to catch the various aspects of the sunlight, which dipped its golden fingers into the silk as though to feel whether this were not the very identical blue texture with which heaven's vault is tapestried. When she had moved to right and left, the pretty girl with the collars and cuffs paused midway between the two extremities, and with a little yearning sigh uttered an "Oh my!" so expressive that it forthwith brought to her side a young man who was passing that way, closely preceded by a cigar.

This youth may have been good or bad, dear Madam, or like the pretty girl herself he may have stood half-way between the two extremities; but anyhow he had a taste for beauty in all its developments, whether human or artificial; and so, glancing from the pretty girl to the dress, and from the pretty dress back again to the girl, he said:

"That gown is the exact colour of your "eyes, missy, and it seems made on purpose for "you."

The girl glanced at him and shook her little head ruefully: "Oh, no, it wasn't made for me," she answered, transferring her basket from one arm to the other because of the weight; "no one would ever think of such a gown for me."

The young man laughed, for he had a subtle sense of humour like the rest of us. "Supposing *I* "bought the gown for you," he proceeded, scrutinising the pretty girl's dress of black merino, and the

modest shawl and bonnet that matched therewith;
"supposing *I* gave you the gown and told you to
"wear it, and bought you another still finer when
"you grew tired of that one? But first tell me what
"your name is."

"My name's Matilda, but they call me Tilly,"
answered the pretty girl; "and I should never grow
"tired of that gown—never," added she, looking
again wistfully at the dress as if the blue of her
eyes and that of those silk folds were in some way
sisters, and not to be parted; moreover the gown
appeared to be smiling at her, and to be saying by
means of those bunches of flowers: "*Forget me not,*
"*Tilly, forget me not!*"

"The truth is, Miss Tilly," observed the young
man, lowering his complimentary voice to a murmur,
"dresses like that were made to match with tresses
"like yours; it's part of the scheme of nature,"
then holding out his hand: "Supposing you put
"down your basket and come into the shop with
me."

Now Tilly had never heard of the scheme of
nature, but she knew something about the scheme
of her collars and cuffs which were to be delivered
in certain houses at appointed hours, so she held
back a moment on the shop's threshold, and, whilst

she was thus holding back there came along at a slouching pace a curate of her parish, the Reverend Agnew Lambe. Mr. Lambe's mind was generally scattered over an area of meditation about soup-tickets and Dorcas clubs, and he could not rally enough of it to reason over the condition of his hats and boots, which were chronically out of repair; but seeing his parishioner he said with affectionate abstraction: "Always busy as a bee, Tilly—what "brings you to this grand shop?" and Tilly answered unabashed, but glancing round her for the young man, who seemed somehow to have vanished in a cloud of his own cigar-smoke at contact with the curate: "There is a gentleman who was going to "give me that blue silk dress in the window."

The curate started, and brought to bear the hundredth part of his mind on this subject, the other ninety and nine being concentrated on a soup-ticket which there was cause to fear had been un-worthily bestowed. "I am afraid you would have "had to pay for that dress, Tilly," he said, dreamily. "No, why should I, since the gentleman was going "to give it me?" exclaimed Tilly in wonder, and a little rebelliously. "There are gifts which cost dear, "and you would have paid for this one in tears, my "child," repeated the curate, with difficulty restrain-ing that hundredth part of his mind from scattering

after the others, and he added quickly, while it was
yet in him to see this point: "If you want a dress
"like that, Tilly, be good and work, work, work!"
and he reiterated "work" with some sorrow, for it
was painful to him to think that if the unmeriting
recipient of the soup-ticket had but plied a trade
industriously he would not now be eating of the
public bounty.

So Tilly hung her head, and went to distribute
her collars and cuffs; then turned home thinking of
what the curate had said, and marvelling why the
complimentary young man had vanished. She was
a good little thing, who did her work better and
more silently than her companions, and would sit
for minutes and minutes making stitches with her
sewing-machine no more noisily than a mouse. She
thought much of that blue sik dress. From the
morning, when its flowers seemed to whisper, *Forget
me not*, *Forget me not*, there was no forgetfulness
possible, and every *tick-tack* of the sewing-machine
was so much melody in her ears, for *tick*, *tack*
sounded much like *work*, *work;* and *work*, *work*
was the recipe which Mr. Lambe had emphatically
given for earning the blue dress in course of
time.

It was very soothing to be able to trust wholly
in the Reverend Agnew Lambe. There are some

who, probing the matter as it were, might have tried
to recall instances of goodness and industry being
publicly rewarded by the gift of a blue dress with
lace trimmings; but Tilly was content to accept the
curate's word, and to conclude that since there was
so much punishment going about for those who went
astray, some Providence was surely abroad which
gave suitable rewards to the deserving, and no reward
would be more suitable than a blue silk dress. Accordingly Tilly grew economical—Economy being a
handmaiden to Goodness—and she faithfully put by
in a box one penny a-day out of thirty-six pence she
earned, which made £ 1 10s. 5d. every twelvemonth.
At this rate it was positive that if she persevered she
might amass sufficient to buy the dress (which cost
no more than fifty guineas or so) by the time she
was eight and forty years old, which was encouragement enough for any girl, but then Tilly left her
goodness out of account, and it was evident that
Goodness, being superior to Economy, ought to yield
more in the end than one penny a day, which
made the prospect doubly or trebly encouraging.

It happened, however, that Tilly's figures did not
marshal themselves into addition sums quite so easily
as is done in ledgers. When her goodness came into play her economy was often at a loss, so that the
two things became as the globes of a sand-glass—

when one was full the other was empty. Thus Tilly, having saved a shilling, met a beggar on a crutch, who requested just that sum to help him dine, whereat Economy whispered, "That's a greedy beggar, "give him nothing;" but Goodness speaking on the other side suggested, "Give him a penny;" and Self-esteem intervening in the dialogue remarked, "It "looks mean to ask a beggar for change;" so the beggar hobbled off with the entire twelvepence. As it was one of the coins wanted for her own day's expenses that Tilly had so recklessly given away, she was obliged to go back to her box and take out the savings, and then she started afresh on an empty box, and with a purpose nowise dashed of accumulating pennies. But when sixty more days had passed and brought their five dozen pence, who should fall ill but Tilly's best friend, and what should the doctor do but order grapes, which Tilly went and bought, the friend being unable; and after this some neighbour's small boy cut a front tooth and took a liking for barley-sugar, which his mother and other kinsfolk pronounced more wholesome for him than his own thumbs. Wherefore Tilly went buying barley-sugar as she had gone and bought grapes; and another neighbour's child having a birthday a doll and some apples came into request, to say nothing of warm socks for a cripple, tea for an old woman who ought to have known better, and multitudinous other taxes to which Tilly's charity seemed to become liable more and more every day, and which she never sought to evade. In short it came to this, that so fast as Economy dropped a penny inside Tilly's box, Goodness came with a stealthy finger and fished it out, so that the blue dress with the lace trimmings appeared to dance away out of sight like a Will-o-' the-wisp, always visible but never to be caught.

Nevertheless Tilly did not despair, and when it chanced that she met Mr. Lambe, that curate brought a section of his straggling mind to bear upon her case, and said kindly, "Work and be good, Tilly; "work, work, work!" and to all this Tilly would reply, "I sometimes work until I am so tired," and saying this would smile and sigh gently as if the blue dress were sadly long coming. In this wise months glided by, and others after them, till one day it came to pass that Tilly fell ill in her turn. The summer with its ripe fruit, leafy trees, mown hay, and song of birds, had arrived then; and it was on a radiant evening full of warmth and perfume that someone came and pulled the Reverend Agnew Lambe by the sleeve and said, "Tilly's ill, and wants to see "you." The curate's mind was far away at that minute among fields and fresh grass, whither he hoped to take London children with buns in their mouths in vanfuls some day next week by public subscription; but he summoned back all his truant thoughts by an effort, and muttered, "Tilly ill!" "Very ill," answered the person, and the curate hastened.

A room with its one window open, and its white curtains forming a framework to the rich sky beyond, a little white bed and Tilly propped up by pillows, over which her golden hair fell in pale cascades. The setting sun streaming through the window seemed to touch her with infinite compassion, and had put the lightest pink glow on her wasted features. When Mr. Lambe entered with his unkempt head bared, she made him a sign to come quite close that she might speak in his ear because her voice was weak, and then whispered, "I am glad—very "glad—you prevented me from taking that dress." "You will soon be well, Tilly," answered the curate, softly, with not one faculty of his mind astray now —not one. "Yes, soon well," murmured Tilly; "and "do you know, I think I shall soon have the blue "dress—very soon, this evening. When I close my "eyes I see them bring it me. Look!" and she laid her hand languidly on his, "they are carrying it to "me now, thousands and thousands of them, all "beckoning to me, and it's so blue—a heavenly blue; "and something whiter on it than lace—white wings;

"it's too beautiful for me." "Not too beautiful for "you, Tilly," muttered the curate; and she smiled, closing her eyes again.

That is how Tilly got her sky-blue dress.

No. 20.—The Women's Club War.

EVER since the time of Eve, not to go too far
back, ladies have got the upper hand of man when
they chose; and they have chosen regularly. Dalilah
may be instanced as a lady who obtained mastery
by diplomatic process; Judith as a lady who asserted
her will with truly feminine force; and both examples
are so typical of the alternative policies which ladies
will adopt when they have set their minds on a
point, that churchwardens may decide at no distant
date to hang pictures of Samson and Holophernes
in every vestry throughout these realms. Bride-
grooms and other feeble folk will then be reminded
by the sight of the man who lost his hair and the
man who lost hair and head together, that resistance
to feminine influence is in a manner undesirable,
and they will attach but a secondary importance to
the vows of obedience made to them under the inspiration of orange flower blossoms.

We have got so far with our narrative, and were

proceeding with the strange tale of a man who went to battle with his wife about a milliner's bill, and was routed with loss, when the newspapers opportunely brought us the account of the "Women's Club War," which has just been commenced in London on the plan of the Whisky War in the United States. Everybody in town has heard of the first desperate engagement in this campaign, which threatens to be so long, and, to all seeming, so successful; but for the benefit of our readers at the North Pole we subjoin a minute account of the whole affray. It offers too valuable a sample of woman's power and endurance to be lightly thrown aside; and the reader is requested to digest it carefully.

On the 30th of last February, then, an extraordinary meeting was held by fifteen cabfuls of the Shrieking Sisterhood, who drove up to a Quakers' place of worship, and swamped a dozen young Quakeresses who had congregated together to discuss the sins of the times. The Quakeresses had gathered by appointment; the Shrieking Sisters came uninvited, but were welcomed nevertheless, and told to sit quiet till the Spirit moved them to say something. They were moved very soon, and all stood up to speak at once; but three of them, who could not get a hearing amid the din, and who declined to see why they should not be allowed to speak first

like the rest, had fits, and were carried out squealing, to be doctored with jugs of cold water. Harmony
being then restored, Dr. Eureka Yelle, late of Utah,
U.S., held forth about matrimony, and looked as if
she were going to make a night of it; but the others,
who wanted to be voting resolutions, screamed at
her, and gradually brought her to the point, which
was this: that club-life must be attacked in front,
rear, and flank, just like the Yankee Whisky Stills.
Clubs are more pernicious, indeed, than Whisky
Stills. From the latter men can be drawn out by
the sleeves of their coats, or by the ears, when need-
ful for their welfare; but into clubs no woman ever
yet penetrated. They were places of wantonness
and perdition, of late hours, light talk, profane games,
and unholy drinks, and what general effects they
produced on the male mind was testified by one of
the young Quakeresses, Sister Phœbe, who wore a
grey silk dress. Phœbe was fair to look upon, and
hence was naturally viewed with mistrust by the
majority of the meeting, who were not fair; but
when Dr. Eureka was at length prevailed upon to
sit down (under loud protest), Phœbe stood up and
thus spake, reddening at first, but growing bold by
degrees: "I am minded that one of my mother's
"kinsmen, being a sojourner in our house, did smoke
"a pound of cigars within a week, and said it was

"his club that taught him so to do. His name is
"Frank Lawless, and he weareth more perfume on
"his handkerchief than the matter requireth, though
"it smelleth nice. But last winter we reasoned one
"among the other that he would take my cousin
"Dinah to wife, for he kissed her under a branch
"of mistletoe, she being a maiden, and he unwedded.
"But when I questioned him on this head, lo! he
"answered that he had kissed her because it pleased
"him, seeing that her cheeks were like peaches; and
"when I further inquired whether it was at his club
"that he had learned these ways, he answered yea,
"and that he would kiss me too if I spake much
"longer."   Here Phœbe blushed under her little
poke-bonnet, Dr. Eureka took snuff, and the rest of
the meeting turned up their eyeballs. "And now,"
pursued Phœbe, with voice steady again, "now I
"would urge that we redeem my kinsman from the
"bonds of sin, wherein his club holdeth him. Since
"Christmas we have not seen him, though my mother
"bade him to tea, and purposed wrestling with him
"in spirit if he had come. But he stayed away,
"and behold! his club is Black's, in St. James's
"Street."

·   This speech of Phœbe's and some other harangues
that supplemented it, formed the preliminaries to
the Grand Demonstration which took place on the

very morrow against Black's Club. Note that Black's
was only selected by accident as the first seat of
operations. The object was and is to put down all
clubs by virtue of that prime right of Woman to
know what man does with his leisure hours; and
there was some talk at first of holding a prayer-
meeting with doleful dirges on the steps of the
Carlton in order to strike at once at the root of the
evil by assailing the most powerful club of any. But
Dr. Eureka Yelle decided, with wise stateswoman-
ship, not to give a political colour to the impressive
social movement. The Carlton would have its turn
like the rest as soon as the Anti-Club League should
be strong enough to let loose one overwhelming flood
of prayers and dirges upon clubs of every size, hue,
and weight; but, meanwhile, it was better to begin
with an establishment which was politically neutral,
and not too big.

That is why Black's was favoured, as abovesaid,
with the first brunt of a Demonstration which com-
prised many hundreds of agitated females, who
marched down St. James's Street in determined rows
of twelve towards dinner-time. Be sure all the Parliamentary agitators for Women's Rights were at their
posts to watch and applaud this moral sight. Mr.
Forsyth, and the Messrs. Bright, John and Jacob,
followed the procession from afar in cabs; others

stood in the windows of Boodle's; and Mr. Disraeli, who is known to favour the movement, and to be musing how he may convert his followers to it, had asked leave to stand on the roof of the Conservative Club armed with a field-glass.

So the procession moved down the street, sweeping on the mob of dirty little boys with it, just as a mighty torrent sweeps weeds, and it reached Black's, where there was a halt, and some scared members thrust their heads out of the windows wondering what was up. They were soon to know. Imparting energy to herself with a pinch of snuff, Dr. Eureka Yelle strode resolutely over the threshold, beat back the hall-porter with her umbrella, and marched into the dining-room, closely followed by the toughest of the Shrieking Sisters, who had been sucking jujubes all through the streets to clear their lungs and throats for action. The men who were dining uttered cries of dismay, and rose with their napkins in their hands, an astonished group; but one fat member who was hard of hearing and had his back turned, went on with his dinner, and Dr. Eureka Yelle dipped his head into his soup-plate to teach him manners. All this was accomplished with the promptitude of an explosion. The fat member had not had time to dry his face, nor the other men to make a guess at their predicament, before Dr. Eureka had shrieked, "Let us pray," and instantly there up-rose a thumping of knees on the carpet, and a con-cert of earnest howls, such as made all the wine-glasses jingle, and cause two dozen bottles of fer-mented liquors to blow their corks straight off in desperation. Through the passages, all over the front hall, and down into the street, was the noise caught up, gathering beautifully in force like the wilder notes of a church organ. The waiters put their fingers into their ears and roared for the police; but we live in a free country, and the police fled. The fat member, who had had his head dipped into the soup, retreated into a corner and shouted for some ice to bathe his face with; but the din rose and rose, and above it all towered the squalls of Dr. Eureka Yelle, who, in chorus with her Sisters, declared herself a miserable sinner—a fact which none there controverted.

But into this scene of piety had crept with the rest Sister Phœbe, who knelt near one of the tables with her little chin close to a dish of early asparagus. She tried to keep her eyes on the ground, but they roamed about in search of her kinsman, Frank Law-less, and when they had found him they stared with some marvel to see this unregenerate youth was not stirred to much humility by the penitential wails that were being gasped forth for his behoof. Nay, when his first surprise had subsided, his attitude was one of flippancy, and judge how Phœbe marvelled when she beheld him impatiently catch up a bowl, advance towards Dr. Eureka Yelle, and thus address her:—"Madam, you claim all the rights of "our sex?" "Yes!" shrieked Dr. Eureka, interrupting her prayer. "Well, then you shall enjoy its "privileges—the privilege of being dealt with sum- "marily when it becomes offensive. Move away, "please, or I'll empty this bowl of lobster sauce over "your head." "Help! you're a brute!" yelped Dr. Eureka, opening her umbrella, and making a tent of it; but she was not in immediate danger, for, on second thoughts, Mr. Frank Lawless paused with his bowl uplifted, and sang out to his friends, "Catch "up sauces and vegetables, all of you; but let us "only fling them at the old and ugly ones. We give "the young ones five minutes to skedaddle!" Five minutes! Less than that was required; for as those words "old" and "ugly," which are as molten lead on women's ears, dropped on the concourse, all of the Sisters, who, shrivelled and angular, dry, unlovable and loveless—and they formed the bulk as they ever do in such throngs—lifted up their voices, scrambled to their beetle-crushing feet, and ran over each other in a fine helter-skelter down the staircase. Mr. Disraeli and the two Messrs. Bright, John

and Jacob, saw them pelt away up by-streets, and
were struck by their wondrous agility; but the main
essential was that the dining-room at Black's was
cleared—for it was not till a few minutes had elapsed
that someone noticed the presence of one praying
Sister, who had tarried behind after all the others
had vanished, and this one was Phœbe.

She had not availed herself of the five minutes'
grace granted to the pretty ones, and there she knelt
in a corner, close to the dish of early asparagus.
"Hullo! Phœbe, what are you doing in such com-
"pany;" asked Mr. F. Lawless, as he recognised her
with astonishment, and approached her. "Didn't
"you hear what we just threatened?" "Yea, I
"heard thee," she replied, "and thou mayest pour
"the lobster-sauce over my head if thou pleasest,
"but I will abide here till I have converted thee."
There was no pouring lobster-sauce over Phœbe; so
her kinsman delicately stooped, lifted her off her
knees, and carried her into another room and to a
seat, then said: "Verily thou canst convert me,
"Phœbe, by wearing a bonnet with flowers in it,
"and a brighter-coloured dress; also by letting me
"kiss thee," and he kissed her without waiting for leave.
"Nay," said she, in confusion, "but thou did'st kiss
"my cousin Dinah." "Yea," answered he, gravely,
"but it was not so nice as in thy case; and now,

"Phœbe, wilt thou wear the flowers?"　"What "flowers?" inquired Phœbe, with her eyes downcast. "Orange-flower blossoms," suggested Mr. Frank, in a whisper, and Phœbe's reply came demurely enough, "Dost thou think they would convert "thee?" . . . . .

No. 21.—La Rosière.

In the French village of Trie-les-Charmes it is
the custom of the Municipal Council to meet once
a year, and to lay hands—figuratively speaking—on
the most virtuous girl of the commune. The parish
priest, who, through the confessional, possibly knows
more about rustic virtue than all the councillors,
and even the councillors' wives, tied together, is not
allowed to be present at the debate; and this on a
principle, prevalent in other countries beside France,
that those who know too much should be kept outside. However, the councillors judge of virtue by
such lights as are common to us all; and if they
fail to agree they hint opprobrious things about one
another's private lives, as is done in higher as-
semblies. When at length they have shouted enough
to come to an understanding, they fall to voting by
means of bits of paper dropped into a box, and
the girl who gets most votes is elected Rosière. On
a summer Sunday they take her in pomp to the

village church; they set a crown of white roses on
her head, give her a gold watch, a pair of earrings,
a sum in money, a champagne breakfast, and a
ball; and she thus starts fair in life with the notion
that to the virtuous this world offers an unbroken
series of balls, champagne breakfasts, gold trinkets,
and bank-notes to their career's end.

Now, one being in that village of Trie-les-
Charmes, and musing over British virtue, a thing I
dearly love, I sauntered down the main street, and
came upon three maidens washing table linen in
three tubs placed on the thresholds of three cottages. One of them had hard eyes and firm lips,
and beat down her washing-bat with loud sounding
thwacks on her napkins, as if these were un-virtuous
textures that needed correction; the second squinted;
the third—well, the third was not fair to look upon;
and I learned without surprise that she was the
most promising among the candidates for the roses
and the breakfast, for on her immaculate virtue I
would have wagered my hat and my boots. I would
have staked the rest of my clothing that the other
two maidens were virtuous also; nor could I see
any reason why they should not remain so as long
as it suited them, for I knew the young men of
Trie-les-Charmes to be Frenchmen of excellent taste.
So smiling respectfully at the three washing-girls, as

I might have done at three bottles of wine that had
never been tried, at three British volunteers who
had never seen action, or at three Radical Irishmen
who had never been invited to Court, I strolled onwards past the village café, the Mairie, the flocks of
Gallic cocks and hens strutting in the sun, past the
gendarme with yellow baldrick, taking note of a
pig who was trespassing, and so into the fields,
where soon I espied a girl kneeling under shelter
of a hedge, and heaping up stones into a mound
with her hands. A brook babbled hard by, a
water-mill tossed its cascades with a foaming noise,
and this drowned the voice of the girl, for I could
see she was speaking to herself. I approached, and
then perceived that a basketful of flowers was lying
beside the stone mound, and that on the mound itself was seated, as if drunk, an ugly wooden doll,
dressed in muslin, and wearing a crown of rosebuds
set a-cock on its head. The unfortunate figure's
arms were stretched out starkly, its legs straggled
outwards, its bust was bent, and of all the dis-
sipated-looking dolls I had ever beheld, this one's
case was certainly the worst. It made me laugh
aloud, after the civil manner of tourists, and then I
glanced at the girl, who had started up, and was
staring at me with large, hazel eyes, circling like a
wild gazelle's. She was undeniably the handsomest

girl I had seen in Trie-les-Charmes or its neighbourhood. Her dark hair fell in rippling curls over
her white neck, her lips were ripe with cherry blood,
her cheeks pink as May roses, and she was dressed
in a blue and white gown of printed cotton, looped
·up over a scarlet petticoat, her feet being cased in
wooden shoes, and her shoulders covered with an
orange neckerchief. When we had both sufficiently
reconnoitred each other—

"What is your name, Mademoiselle?" said I.

"Isabelle Brune," replied she, mistrustfully.

"And I will be bound they call you 'Belle
"Brune.'"

"Yes, they do."

"That shows more sense than I dared hoped of
"them. But may I ask what you are doing with
"that ugly doll?"

What she was doing could be no business of
mine; but the courtesy of the British tourist as
abovesaid never falters. She blushed, and taking
me perhaps for some official Frenchman whose
questions require answering, she stood on the tips
of her wooden shoes and peeped over the hedge, to
see that there were no listeners. Then looking
shyly at the doll, she murmured, "To-morrow, you
"see, the Rosière is to be elected."

"And you are one of the candidates?"

13*

"Yes, I am; and everybody knows if you take "the likeness of the girl whom you want to be the "winner, and set her on a little altar like this one, "crowning her with roses, and praying to the Virgin "for an hour, you will have what you wish."

I remembered a pious superstition, which consisted in sticking needles into the presentment of your enemy in order that evil might light upon him and his seed; but I had heard of no recipe for doing good to one's friends, perhaps because the applicants for such recipes have ever been few. But it was evident that in this instance the friend whom Belle Brune desired to benefit was herself, so I laughed again, and drawing out my pocket-book, said: "The Powers who can grant your prayer, "Mademoiselle, will never accept that doll as an "image of yourself. Sit down under the hedge, "and let me sketch a better portrait of you. We "will put it on the mound and crown it together."

"Oh, no! you have not understood me," she exclaimed, lifting both her hands before her face, and making a few steps back. "Mon Dieu! that doll is "not me—it's Marie Rougeaud."

"It's Marie Rougeaud? Do you mean then that "you are a candidate for the Rosière's crown and "do not want to win?"

"Mon Dieu! Monsieur," she said, piteously, "it's

"very cruel to ask me so many questions. How can
"I know that you won't go and repeat everything I
"say?"

"I shall repeat nothing. You may trust me."

"Bien vrai! Well, then," said she, standing
once more on tiptoe to peep over the hedge, and
blushing now to a deeper red—"Well, then, I am
"almost certain to be elected, because my uncle is
"Mayor and Claude Riant, my lover, is one of the
"council. But Claude knows I ought not to be
"elected, only when I told him he laughed and
"said I should have the watch and the things
"whether I liked it or not. You know, though,
"Monsieur, that if a girl wears the Rosière's crown
"without having a right to it, misfortune falls upon
"her: it's written in the books, and the curé said so
"last Sunday in his sermons, making me cry. So I
"came out here with the doll, which is meant for
"Marie Rougeaud. You know Marie—who supports
"her father and her young brothers and sisters, for
"her mother died last harvesting? She is a girl
"who deserves to be Rosière; and there is a gift of
"money which she will spend better than I would.
"It would burn my fingers."

"Is Mary Rougeaud the crooked girl with the
"squint whom I saw washing at her door when I
"came by?" I inquired, when astonishment, or

some other feeling, had subsided enough to let me speak, which was not immediately.

"Marie is not pretty," rejoined Belle Brune, "simply; but this morning she came to me and said: "'You must let me make the gown you will wear "on the day when you are crowned, Belle; I will "make it better than any one else: they none of "them love you as I do.' That's what she said, and "these things go to a girl's heart, Monsieur. I wish "the lightning had come and killed me then."

"The lightning will not come and kill you," I answered; "and look here, Mademoiselle, if I had "to elect the Rosière after what you have told me, "I would choose you. You can wear the crown "safely; it will never bring you misfortune."

Saying this I cleared the hedge and walked homewards—rather rapidly as it appeared to me, and wondering what was the mist that had suddenly sprung up and made Belle Brune seem dim to me as she stood on the hedge-bank, gazing after me with eyes wide open and lips slightly quivering.

The next day I heard that Belle Brune had been elected Rosière; and that Monsieur le Curé had given a great leap when apprised of the fact. I was not concerned as to whether he leaped or not, for the election pleased me well, and on Rose-Sunday the curious observer might have seen me conspicuous in

the throng which lined the church-porch ready to
cheer the maid of virtue. Slowly and triumphantly
Belle Brune came down the village street leaning on
the arm of the Mayor girt with his silken sash, and
preceded by the clashing music of the Firemen's
band. Behind her walked the Rosières of previous
years, some married, and leading their toddling
children by the hand; behind these, three in a row,
marched the Municipal Councillors, with Claude
Riant, Belle's lover, very brave with a bright button-
hole nosegay. More firemen in uniform closed the
procession, and amidst cheers, showers of rose-leaves
and waving of handkerchiefs, the Rosière passed
through the porch into the church, where the organ
softly pealed her welcome. How the curé preached,
or whether he preached, I did not care to notice,
but I watched Belle Brune kneel at the altar and
receive her crown of roses, her earrings, and her
watch and chain from the Prefect's wife, who played
the part of Patroness; then the beadle, clanging his
halbert on the flags, went round the church with
Madame la Prefête, who made a collection on Belle
Brune's behalf, and money had never chinked so
musically in my ears as when I heard it now drop
by driblets of gold and silver into the velvet bag.
Before the service was over it was being whispered
that what with the municipal gift and the subscrip-

tions the dowry would amount to 3000 francs, for many visitors had come from Paris; and so I understood, ay, and sympathised with the elate look of Claude Riant as he escorted his future bride to the champagne breakfast after the church service. But Belle Brune was pale, and going by me she cast me a wistful glance, and seemed to reproach me for the cheer which I gave her with all my heart, standing bareheaded.

I heard the revellers carouse in the Mairie far into the afternoon, whilst wine-corks popped, and toasts were cried with all the gay hubbub of French folk making holiday. Outside there was a fair, and when the Rosière's health was drunk the buyers and sellers at the booths caught up the cheer which came ringing to them through the open windows; and a crowd of village boys and girls hurried joyfully by, carrying a May bough, which was to be planted according to usage outside the Rosière's house. So the afternoon wore on, the shadows deepened in the church porch and under the eaves of the cottages, and the banqueting people, flushed and merry, separated to prepare for the ball of the evening. At this hour the booth people began to light their lanterns; and it may have been an hour after the dusk had fairly set in that, roaming on the outskirts of the fair, I saw a muffled figure of a girl in a

grey cloak, and with a hood drawn over her face, flit with quick steps through the blaze of booth illuminations, and vanish into the darkness down the road which led to the Paris railway station. I should not have remarked the incident but for the fact that white shoes and the edge of a white dress peeped under the girl's cloak; and puzzling out this mystery I made my way back to the part of the village where Belle's house lay. All was quiet here; but suddenly, even as I stood, a frightened cry was raised, figures rushed to and fro, and in a moment a throng was collected, and a babel of voices lifted up astonished exclamations. What could be the matter? I hastened forward, and found myself in a crowd, which was straining its eyes to see into a cottage—not Belle's—where Claude Riant was gesticulating, whilst a scared girl with dismal features was pointing to some objects on the table. It was Marie Rougeaud's cottage. I walked in, and saw that the things on the table were Belle Brune's crown of roses, her watch and earrings, and her purseful of money. They had been left there, no one knew by whom, or when; but beside them was a hurried note:—
"These things are yours, Marie, and you must for-
"give me; but I did my best. I thought I should
"have cried aloud in the church. God bless you,
"and good-by. Your unhappy—BELLE."

Claude Riant, who staggered out of the cottage, and I, who wended my way home moodily, were probably the only two who comprehended the matter just then, though tattle and scandal were busy enough on the morrow. Belle Brune had gone to Paris to seek service, and she never appeared in her village again. Her name was, of course, struck off the list of Rosières; and yet it somehow seems to me that on the tablet where the names are inscribed in letters of gold, hers, in despite of the erasure, stands out more brightly and purely than any of the others.

No. 22.—A Sympathetic Couple.

IT is known that our Queen counts some two hundred million subjects, not reckoning those for dissatisfaction with the conduct of the Irish. Among this mass of persons many who have thoughtful minds must have been chagrined before now at the curious waywardness shown by the public in the bestowal of its sympathies. If the public firmly declined to sympathise with anybody, one could understand the feeling; but to allot one's sympathies year after year, and century after century, to the wrong people, is behaviour of a puzzling sort. Take, for instance, the sympathies so freely lavished upon Abraham, Agamemnon, and Idomeneus, for their readiness to sacrifice Isaac, Iphigenia, and little Idomeneus, respectively. Having myself known sundry fathers who were ready to sacrifice, not only their sons and daughters, but their wives, aunts, and everybody else who stood in the way of their profit or comfort, I can never read of the alacrity evinced by Abraham, Agamemnon, and Idomeneus without being moved to much sympathy for Isaac, Iphigenia, and little Idomeneus. Similarly, as regards the Brutus, who sent his sons to the scaffold, and Ugolino, who ate his, one of the few things taught me at an expensive school was to pity Brutus, and to commiserate Ugolino; and yet, after giving the matter twenty years' reflection, it strikes me that the distress of these model fathers was more than matched by that of the sons who were beheaded, and that of the sons who were eaten, even though you make every allowance for the comfort of the latter at knowing that their father only ate them that they might be spared the pain of seeing so affectionate a parent die of hunger. We next come to the case of Tarquin and Lucretia, and here I would not be thought to discourage any virtuous lady of our own time who might wish to act as Lucretia did; nevertheless one may submit that the position of wretched Tarquin, who had stumbled upon a pretty woman so exceptionally melodramatic, was not one to be envied. And if we will only compare ancient things with modern, it may be fairly asked again whether the keen sympathy displayed by all of us for Captain Potiphar's young friend would be awarded to any nowaday Mr. Joseph, who should bounce unpolitely out of a Belgravian boudoir, leaving his overcoat behind him. But *incedo per ignes.* . . . .

All I mean to say is that sympathy should not be, like soup-tickets or Liberal peerages, bestowed on people who have wrought little to deserve the same. It should be conferred after a judicious appraising of the merits of the claimants; and I am so much imbued with this opinion, that I lately had it printed on thin hand-bills, and stood at the foot of the Duke of York's column, distributing them to all who came near to admire that work of art. I had not been so occupied above a week, when a sorry-looking man shambled by, took one of my bills, and trudged down the steps; but half way he paused, leaned against the iron baluster, and fixing his eyes on my handbills, raised a series of such sorrowful snivels that I was by his side in an instant. With infinite caress I stroked the nap of his hat, and led him down to the place in the Mall where they sell milk. But he refused to be comforted, and—

> " The big round tears
> Coursed one another down his innocent nose
> In piteous chase."

It was only when he had drank about a sixpenn'orth of milk and refused to pay for it, on the ground that he never took anything between his meals, that I at last ventured to say—

"Your ways are peculiar, but it seems to me that "you are a dejected man in search of sympathy."

"Yes, that's it," said he, spreading his wet handkerchief over my head to dry. "Such as you see
"me, I am rich but honest; my ancient family have
"sat in the House of Lords for more than a year
"and a half, and a hundred thousand people come
"and knock at my door every afternoon."

"Come—a hundred thousand!" said I, with gentle
reproof.

"Well, at least three or four people do!" cried
he, in anger; "but we shall never get on if you pin
"me down to a figure more or less," and he profited
by my contrition to exchange his umbrella for my
own, because mine was newer; then he proceeded:
"And not one of those hundred and fifty thousand
"will bless me with a word of sympathy, so that
"often I wish I could stow them all inside one omni-
"bus, and that the sea would swallow them up as
"Jonah did the whale."

"That is a sentiment which I cannot approve,"
said I, interrupting him. "It is as outrageously mis-
"placed as a poached egg on one's shirt front."

"Don't go on like that till you've heard the rest
"of my story," he screamed, jamming his gloves into
my mouth with his thumbs; "why what shall you
"say when I tell you that those two hundred thou-
"sand men of all sizes come to make love to my
"wife? Moidora her name is, and I married her last

"year hoping she would devote herself to me night "and day. But she despises me with all her soul. "When I left home she refused to come out, saying "that she was going to receive all the Tory mem- "bers of the House of Commons in the back draw- "ing-room."

"All the Tory members!" I ejaculated, spitting out the gloves and flinging them to one of the cows, who swallowed them.

"Well, he is the biggest member on the Tory "side," raved the stranger, appropriating my own gloves to replace his, and stamping on my foot to draw my attention elsewhere. "Moidora made her- "self smart to welcome him. She came down in "a new primrose dress with an asparagus in her "hair."

"An asparagus?"

"Well, call it a moss-rose if you like; but leave "me alone. Last week she put five hundred pounds' "worth of oyster-shells round her neck to give tea "and muffins to all the Liberal members."

"I cannot accept that version as accurate," I an- swered, with a grimness that surprised me, as I stooped and looked for my gloves. "Judging by the "loose way in which you talk I should take those "oyster-shells to be pearls, and I should estimate the

"number of Liberal members at something between
"one and two."

"How many would you have?" he replied, with
both eyes glaring. "Are you such a brute as not to
"sympathise with a man who sees his wife kissed
"and his tea drunk by the two great parties in the
"State?"

I gave him a hard rap on the head with the
handle of his umbrella, because his attitude was
menacing; and whilst he was rubbing his pate, I
replied—

"So far my sympathies are all on the side of
"your wife. When the cat goes mousing I infer
"that she is not pleased with the food at home; when
"a pretty woman has the two great parties in the
"State to tea, I conclude that she is not contented
"with her husband, and that is your fault. Besides,"
added I, remembering how a stranger had once
hoaxed me with the story of a Life-Guardsman;
"besides, I have a notion that the Tory member
"must be Mrs. Moidora's grandfather, and the Li-
"berals her cousins, once or twice removed—from
"office."

He made no rejoinder, and I could see that my
striking argument with the umbrella-handle had
stunned him. I drew out my scarf-pin and pricked
him on the legs to make him speak; but it was of

no use, and when we had sat side by side for hours
and I saw that nothing more was to be got out of
him except grunts and groans, I crushed his hat
over his eyes and went my ways, well-pleased that
he had not cozened me out of the sympathy he
coveted. But for all this I was not wholly satisfied
with my own views about Mrs. Moidora. It seemed
to me that there was a mystery in this lady worth
clearing up, and accordingly I repaired from the
Mall to her house—for I knew the address, her husband being a public character.

A page showed me up to the back drawing-room,
where Mrs. Moidora was pouring out tea for three
men, whose mouths were full of crumpets. There
was a fat Tory member, a yet fatter Liberal, and a
third politician, so small and lean that I set him
down for half a Radical. They all three glared at
me as if I were come for the last crumpet; but as I
had no wish to sit and see that last crumpet
scrambled for by their thirty fingers I hinted gloomily
that an Election Judge and a policeman were waiting
below to question them about bribery, whereat they
stampeded so fast that the Tory and the Liberal got
jammed together in the doorway, which obliged the
half Radical to take frantic butts at them with his
hard skull till they were loosed, roaring. Meanwhile
Mrs. Moidora sat with her arms folded over the

bosom of her primrose dress, and begged to know, firstly, who I was; ninthly, and lastly, why I had come up to her back drawing-room, frightening away the great parties in the State with personal remarks. She was so nice, and spoke so much like a curly-headed baby who means mischief, that I helped myself respectfully to the last crumpet, and raised the lid of the teapot to see whether there were symptoms of another cup—then I told her what were the facts. I had met her husband begging for sympathy at the foot of the Duke of York's column, and it was a marvel to me how she could let the partner of her life thus roam about destitute. She listened with an evident purpose of hysterics, clashing the sugar tongs and the slop-basin together to form a derisive accompaniment to my words, and when at last the crumpet compelled me to pause a moment for breath she leaned forward, and exclaimed—

"Now that you've spoken for a whole day and a "night, perhaps you'll allow a lady to give *her* ver-"sion of her husband's conduct, you unmannerly "person. His name is Enoch, so christened because "'e knocked down all my illusions as to what a ten-"der husband's behaviour should be. What do you "think of a man who vows to cherish you, then "spends forty-eight hours every day at his club, "squanders ten thousand pounds an evening on

"sherry and bitters, and comes in at midnight smok-
"ing cigars as big as the Victoria Tower?"

"I never met with a cigar of that size," was my
emphatic protest.

"You say much more, and I'll make them long
"as Piccadilly!" cried she, with flaming eyes. "Do
"you think I don't know what tobacco is?—when
"everybody is aware that if a woman speaks on
"questions like these you're bound to-back-her!"

"This is too horrible!" I ejaculated, rising to go;
but she pinned me to my seat by holding the tea-
pot at me like a pistol, and swearing to scald my
legs if I made another move.

"You shall hear everything that inhuman wretch
"has done to vex me," declared she, in agitation.
"Yesterday I wanted him to go out with me, so that
"we might both be measured for a new pew at St.
"George's, Hanover Square; but he went out walk-
"ing instead, with his own weight in Bath buns, and
"fed all the ducks and geese in the parks, well
"knowing that I detest water-fowl. No woman was
"ever so aggravated since the time of Semiramis;
"but she made herself even with her husband by
"poisoning him."

"Yes, but that was four thousand years ago,"
murmured I, feeling that she was on a dangerous
incline.

"Four thousand years!" she echoed, mockingly;
"why we are not yet in the nineteenth century, and
"you ought to blush for your ignorance. Semiramis
"married Ninnus; so baptised because he was a
"ninny to marry a Semi-raw-miss who led him by
"the nose; but all men are like that. I know my
"history, for the Tory and Liberal members come
"here to teach me; and to-morrow there'll be five-
"fourths of the Social Science Congress eating tea-
"cakes in this room, because I want to know every-
"thing, and put the men to shame. Last week I
"learned the properties of heat and cold."

"Well, that reminds me that I feel hot, and
"should like to go if you'll take that tea-pot away."

"No: you don't feel hot a bit," she retorted, in-
"dignantly. The property of heat is to dilate bodies,
"that of cold to contract them—as you can see by
"the days, which are long in summer and short in
"winter. If you were hot you would have swollen
"to twice your size; whereas you look much smaller
"than when you first came into the room."

I felt that such a conversation could not be prolonged with profit. I had clearly made a mistake.
I threw myself on her indulgence and on my knees,
declaring in abject terms that every grain of sympathy I possessed was hers thenceforth, and not her
husband's whom I despised. She threw lumps of

sugar at me, and when the basin was empty, poured all the dregs of the teacups into my hat. Eventually she watered me with the teapot, crying out as she did so:—"And who gave you the right to despise "my husband, I should like to know? There'll be "nothing to complain of in him when I've brought "him to do everything I wish. He shall buy me a new "dress three times a week; he shall give up feeding "the water-fowls; I won't allow him cigars, clubs, or "sherry-and-bitters; and when the Whigs and Tories "come here, he shall hand round the muffins and "crumpets for them, because that's my idea of a "happy home." I was still on my knees, so she poured out all the ice and butter out of the butter-boat on to my scalded pate, and added, "As for you "—get along, you're too ugly!"

So I fled, and am now writing these lines with a bread-poultice on my head, convinced that before awarding sympathy in a dispute between man and wife you should hear both sides dispassionately, and stick to the lady's version, if you burst for it.

No. 23.—The Proud Man.

HAVING heard that every road led to Rome, I tried to get to it by the Dorking coach; but on arriving at Horsham, needles and pins in the left leg made me limp down and hobble up and down outside an inn, at the door of which stood a man holding a brown-paper parcel under his arm. He was evidently a proud mán, but the shabbiness of his clothes and the puny proportions of his person assorted so ill with the superciliousness of his mien, that I stared at him a moment, puzzling out what reasons he could possibly have for his pride. Whilst I was so staring the coach went off without me. I hallooed and ran, but the men on the hind seats tossed me an empty strawberry pottle, and by the time I had picked this up and examined it the coach had disappeared round a turning. I came back murmuring, but as there was no cause why I should go to Rome that day, nor indeed why I should go there at all, I looked for the Proud Man, and seeing him enter the Commercial Room of the inn, I followed him.

He may have been thirty or fifty years of age; but the more you considered him the shabbier he seemed. Nobody ever saw such trousers, nor a hat so disdainful of the decencies of this life. He appeared to be unaware of my presence, or contemptuous of it; for paying no heed to an observation of mine about rain being wanted for the new-mown hay, he rang the bell, and when the waiter entered, pointed to his brown-paper parcel, which lay on the table.

"That parcel will be safe in this room?" he asked, gliding for the first time a mistrustful glance in my direction.

"Quite safe, sir," said the waiter, also speeding a glance at me.

"Let there be no equivocation on that subject, "for I mean to leave it here an hour," rejoined the man, deliberately. "And look here—at one, two "ladies will be here—that is, a young lady and her "maid; and they will inquire for ——." He was about to give a name, but, remembering me, fumbled in his waistcoat-pocket for the duskiest visiting card I have ever seen. "They will inquire for the name "on that card. You will show them up to a private

"room, and, as soon as I come in, serve up dinner
"for myself and the young lady—anything you may
"have."

"Roast leg of pork, sir, and a cherry tart."

"That will do, with two quarts of stout," answered the Proud Man, thoughtfully. "As to
"that parcel, you will bring it up with the tart—
"not before. You again assure me it will be
"safe?"

"Quite safe, sir," repeated the waiter. "I will
"look after it myself."

I could not but feel this was an indirect way of
saying that the waiter would look after me; so,
anxious to place myself on a proper footing, I said,
"And I will look after it too." But the Proud Man
let fall on me a smooth glance of complete suspicion,
shrugged his shoulders, and strode out of the
room.

Now my own hat was a new one, and my coat
such as any man would have made a point of un-
hooking from a peg in a club dressing-room and
walking off with, if I had given him the chance. I
was accustomed to be respected on account of that
coat and hat, and therefore the strange behaviour of
the man with the parcel confused my ideas of social
niceties, and filled me with humiliation. What could

he have done to earn so high a notion of himself
and so poor a one of others?—and, then, what could
there be inside that parcel to which he attached
such exaggerated importance? The waiter came in
twice within ten minutes to see whether the parcel
was in its place; but as I ended by ordering something to drink, he concluded that I was one who
could be trusted, and left me alone. I thought long
and tortuously as I stirred my beverage, which was
plain water with some brandy in it; but somehow,
while thinking, I fidgeted in my chair, and every
fidget brought me nearer to the table and the parcel.
By five minutes to one I was so near the parcel that
another fidget would have induced me to stretch out
my hand and feel it. I am not even sure but that
a laudable curiosity would not have prompted me to
investigate its contents in order to be easier in mind
for the rest of the day. But at this juncture there
was a trundling of wheels in the road, and I went
out into the passage to see a fly drive up to the inn,
with the two ladies expected. At the same time
the Proud Man, who had been out for a walk,
brushed through the door without paying attention to the fly, and hastened upstairs three steps at
a time.

Meanwhile the flyman assisted his fares to alight,
and I held my breath because of the indescribable

beauty of the young creature who had got out first.
You never had a glimpse of hair so rich and shining,
eyes so limpid, or lips so unlike anything I can remember just at present. If I had been in search of
two travelling companions for myself and another
man she is the woman I should have kept for myself, and the other man might have taken the maid,
who was old, if he had pleased. The beautiful
young creature, who wore a black silk dress and
blue bonnet, blushed at being gazed at with such
ardour as I was showing. She whispered to the
waiter, and, under his escort, rustled upstairs on
the track of the Proud Man, the maid following
with a band-box and two umbrellas. Soon after,
the leg of pork might have been seen ascending the
staircase; the two quarts of stout came behind in
due course; and by-and-by the procession was closed
by the cherry-tart, with plenty of powdered sugar
on the top. But before taking up the tart the waiter
came into the Commercial Room for the brown-
paper parcel, which he set respectfully on a tray,
with a pair of scissors beside it, to assist the Proud
Man if he should wish to cut the string. He appeared to have become quite obsequious, this waiter;
and when I ventured to ask if he knew anything of
the man to whom the parcel belonged, he replied,
"No, sir; all I know is that he's a-dining in Number

"Four." This was so mysterious that I called for another glass of something to drink, with less plain water in it than before; but whilst I was breaking the sugar moodily with the crusher the mystery was acutely heightened by the loud clatter of hoofs suddenly nearing the house, as if somebody were flying and some other bodies were in pursuit. The waiter rushed out, so did I; and a couple of perspiring horsemen galloping up to the door cried out excitedly to know whether a proud, shabby man, accompanied by a brown-paper parcel, had been seen in these parts? My lips were opening to say yes, and that he was upstairs with the leg of pork, when the waiter elbowed me back and replied, with the coolness of steady practice, "Such a person was "here about three hours ago, gentlemen, and he "went on by the Dorking coach." "Dorking coach! "confound it, we shall miss him!" roared the horsemen, spurring onwards with an explosion of oaths of which I wholly disapproved, and they vanished instantly in a blinding cloud of dust. But the noise of their horses' hoofs was still audible, and I had not yet had time to tax the waiter with his shameless evasion of the truth, when another cavalcade, with more dust, debouched from the same road as the first, and two mounted policemen with their helmets a-cock from emotion reined in, and gasped

questions about a young lady of eighteen, a maid of
fifty, a band-box, and two umbrellas. "Why your'e
"turning your backs to them," answered the obsequious waiter, without a quaver in his voice. "It
"was eleven o'clock when they stopped here for
"something hot to drink, and they went straight
"on to London in a fly. They must be at Constitu-
"tion Hill by this time." The police muttered
broken words, possibly blessings, gave their bridles
a twist, and were gone; simultaneously a bell tinkled
in the hall, and the waiter made a dash for the bar-
parlour, saying, "That's Number Four ringing for
"their bill."

But I checked the man by the cuff of his coat.
He had told lies which needed explanation; and I
drew him, not unresistingly, indeed, but mildly
protesting, into the Commercial Room. There I
addressed him.

"Your regard for facts is not what I could wish;
"but you will please tell me why you deceived four
"men, and gave as many dumb brutes much useless
"labour."

"What I said was by the orders of Number
"Four, sir," answered the man, in the tone of one
who has a fee. He glanced round to see that
nobody could overhear, put a finger on his lips, and
added, "I think it's an elopement, sir."

"An elopement!"

"Or an abduction. The gentleman doesn't look
"much like one who could whistle away such a
"pretty young lady, but they was mighty soft over
"the leg of pork, and when I left them they was
"billing and cooing over the brown paper parcel.
"They've ordered a fly for three o'clock to take 'em
"to Horsham Junction, and it's near that now.
"Please let me go, sir."

I let him go, and finished what remained in my
glass, scooping out the sugar at the bottom with a
spoon, and putting the slice of lemon in my pocket,
so as to let no one clear undue profits. This done
I set the door ajar, and peered for a while through
the opening, surveying the fore-quarters of lamb and
the denuded poultry hanging by hooks from the
hall ceiling. A snug bar was in the corner, and a
girl with a pink bow at her throat was drawing old
ale for a pair of Surrey farmers, with faces like
steaks. Over the brass-hooped barrels of rum and
shrub behind the girl a canary piped blithesomely,
and on the staircase landing a cupboard clock,
eight feet high, repeated *tack-tock* with patient
rhythm.

But I had eyes for none of these things—only
for the Proud Man, if perchance he should come

down alone whilst I was waiting for him. He arrived at last, with the beautiful creature's shawl thrown negligently over his arm; both hands in his pockets, and humming a tune. The fly was at the door, and he made for the porch, intending perhaps to chew a toothpick there till his sweet companion with the blue bonnet was ready. Protruding my head, however, I beckoned to him with my middle finger, and that so significantly that he sauntered towards me. Then, having shut the door behind his heels, I winked.

"Ill-dressed stranger," I began, "it's not my "wish to bring trouble on you, but I shall follow "you about as the dog did Tobias if you don't "answer at least one question—What on earth is it "makes a man of your mean face and figure, and "trousers, so plaguey proud?"

He laughed a quiet laugh, and slid on me another of those cool, contemptuous glances he had bestowed on me before.

"It's a golden rule for happiness," said he, drily, "to marry well and often."

"I have never tried it, and don't see its applica-"tion in this instance."

"I am proud because I have won that beautiful "young thing who came in the fly," he continued, not heeding me. "Other men wooed her by the "gross, but she preferred me, though she has a "bushel of diamonds in her bandbox, which will be "mine to-morrow, please the pigs."

"One question more," I asked, suspiciously. "Did you woo that young creature with your present "coat and hat?"

"I did, because they are the only ones I have," he replied, gravely. "But now, shall I tell you the "secret of this and past successes of mine?—*it all* "*lies in that brown-paper parcel!*"

I would have begged him to be more explicit, but the rustle of the beautiful young creature's silk dress was heard in the hall; and as I have never kept any lady waiting, nor ever shall, I suffered the Proud Man to depart. He went out through the porch, helped the beautiful girl and her maid into the fly, and got in after them. But when the door had been closed a cry was raised that the brown-paper parcel had been forgotten; whereon the waiter raced upstairs, and soon raced back breathless across the hall, holding the precious thing at arm's length. It was passed through the window with every care, the fly-wheels grated round, and the last I saw of the Proud Man was his eye roaming from the brown-paper parcel to me with a queer expression of pity and disdain mingled.

I have never discovered what was inside that brown-paper parcel, and should be much obliged if any of you could tell me.

———————

No. 24.—"Meesther O'Coon."

It is undeniable that men are dependent on one another, for I never yet heard of anyone who could draw his own tooth satisfactorily. Still harder is it for a man to possess himself of a lucrative post, the patronage whereof belongs to someone else who is reluctant to bestow it. It is clear, then, that the first man depends on the second; and, this being so, I was not surprised to find myself climbing the staircase of a Government office one day, intent on asking a minister for a post which I saw no means of filling without his help. I will not detain you by relating with what gratifying alacrity the minister refused my request. Tucking his coat-tails under his arm, he vowed that he could never for one moment think of such a thing; and it further happened that he had no need to think, having just made over the post to an Irishman, who had not been gone five minutes.

"An Irishman with a mouth like a gash?" I

asked, fixing my eyes on the minister's boots, and
running them up slowly over all the articles of his
apparel to his top-knot, which is the surest way I
know to make a man fancy that there is something
wrong with his garments, and to cause him discom-
fort. "A mouth like a gash, splay feet, and named
"Meesther O'Coon?"

"The same man," replied the minister, reddening as he slipped his eye from his waistcoat downwards, to see whether there really was a button un-
fastened, or a shoe-string amiss; "and he snivels,"
added the right honourable gentleman, with some
anger on perceiving that all his buttons and strings
were in the proper condition.

I approached the minister, and laid a forefinger
on the cavity of his waistcoat, reflecting as I did so
that he was as fat a statesman, as one could expect
for the money: "You have given a snug post to a
"man who snivels, and who, by current report, is as
"consummate a bore as any the sister isle ever sent
"abroad, which is saying a great deal. Thereby
"hangs a tale!"

"Thereby hangs a tale," echoed the minister,
eyeing me with aversion, as if I had found him
out; "will you take a glass of sherry and a bis-
cuit?"

"No; but I'll take a post in the Customs and a

"salary." Saying which I sat down and knocked my forefinger archly against my nose. "I know your "secret. If you have appointed Meesther O'Coon "to sit in the room next yours, to come into inter- "course with you hourly and daily, excepting Sun- "day—which is happily a day for church, whither "the Irishman will not follow you—if you have done "that, it is that you don't expect to be in office "long."

"You shall have the post in the Customs, only "speak lower," exclaimed the minister, making a row with the tongs to drown my voice. He was ex- cited, and a bear on a hot-plate dances just as he did on the hearthrug.

"You have said to yourself: 'I will bequeath "Meesther O'Coon as a legacy to my successor,'" I continued, imperturbably. "And for the matter of "that your calculation is a neat one. Your successor "will not be able to stand O'Coon. Sooner than sit "closeted with him, he will leave him to bungle "irresponsibly in that next room; the affairs of the "department will all go wrong, your successor will "bear the blame, and you will be able to pitch into "him from the Opposition benches. You're an old "bird!"

The minister caught up a pen, signed me an appointment in the Customs, and pushed me out of the room by the shoulders. He even leaned over the balusters to see whether I truly went out of the house, which I did honourably. At the door, however, a broken-down general officer, who had been cashiered by some clerk in another department, asked me for twopence to buy himself a dinner, and I thought this was at good opportunity for being generous at little cost—so I gave him my appointment in the Customs, well knowing I should be able to extract another for myself by exercising judicious pressure on that fat minister upstairs. Then it occurred to me that I should like to see Meesther O'Coon, for according to rumour this was not the first piece of promotion, nor the fifth which this Celt had wrested from the Saxon despoiler by the most forcible of all merits—that of making himself unpleasant.

His name was in the Directory. He occupied a big house with some geraniums on the balcony, and I repaired thither, inventing some untruth—I know not what—to obtain admittance. They—that is, a large-eared footman—admitted me on a payment in cash; but Meesther O'Coon was out, and I could only see young Pat O'Coon, who sat in the dining-room taking shots at a Scotch dog with crusts of bread to make the time pass. He was a red-headed boy, with freckles, a flat nose, and a mouth that

could have swallowed anything from a ten-pound
note to a dish of stew without gulping—in fact, the
reduced image of his father. Smiling broadly at
him, but wishing the while that his young nails had
been cleaner, I said—

"The object of my visit was to congratulate your
"father for having obtained a post which I wanted
"for myself."

"Sure, thin, and it's a lie ye can tell when ye've
"the mind," laughed this boy, lifting the Scotch
dog on to the table by his tail, and groping about
with his foot for another dog who lay under a chair,
and whom, by his yelp, I detected for an English
terrier. "What ye've come afther is to ask feayther
"how he got his post, and faith I'll tell ye if ye give
"us a shillin'."

I handed the lad a Swiss franc which had been
palmed off on me by an hotel-waiter, but his inno-
cent eye detected the fraud, and he stipulated immediately for a two-shilling piece under threat of
exposing me. I disbursed the florin, and held out
my hand for the franc, but he kept it, declaring he
should find a use for it. Then, having ducked
under the table and fished up the English dog, he
planted him beside his miserable Scotch compeer,
and gave tongue—

"Feayther and I belong to a down-throdden

"nationalitee, and divil a scruple shall we ever have
"about makin' money out of those who've carried
"off the mate and dthrink from Ould Ireland. Why,
"it's grinnin' I am when I remember that these two
"spalpeen dogs turned up their tails at us at first
"years ago because we were Irish."

"They are civil enough now," I remarked, as
the long suffering terriers, receiving each a fillip on
the nose, jumped howling off the table and ran
under the side-board.

"Yes, for I've bin five years schoolin' thim," said
Pat O'Coon, proudly; "and there's an Irish dog up-
"stairs, true Kilkenny breed, who gits rale bits of
"mate and chicken, while those two there look on
"with wather runnin' out o' their eyes and mouth,
"and only git bones. Well, it's just the same with
"feayther and the English and Scotch clerks in the
"offices."

"Your father only allows them the bones?"

"Yes, more power to him! When he came to
"England with divil a silver piece in the bottom of
"his breeches pockets, which had holes in 'em, he
"said, 'It's well behaved I'll be, so that they'll be
"afther finding no fault with me; but I'll speak cross
"and weep the wrongs of Ould Ireland into their
"ears, so that every mother's son of 'em 'll want to
"see me out o' the way, and that's how promo-

"tion 'll come, like the suvrins into Father O'Raffle's
"fob—bit by bit." This is what feayther said, and
"sorry a man is thare that now turns up his tail at
"him."

"I should not have promoted your father, but
"have sent him back to Ireland with my——bless-
"ing," I replied, with some vehemence.

"Feayther never gave them a chance, the gos-
"soons!" retorted young Pat, with the paternal snivel.
"It would have benefited your sowl to see the way
"he worked, till all those English and Scotch—bad
"luck to their grandmowthers—said, 'O'Coon ud be
"a jewel if it warn't for his temper'—and some of
"these days, when I've a few inches more a-growing
"over mee head, I'll do as feayther did. Faith and
"ye bet on it."

It was very horrible to hear such principles and
pronunciation from a boy of so tender years. He
sat with his legs drawn up under his chair, whistling to the two dogs, and I pondered how I might
remonstrate with him to some purpose. But I had
not mused a minute and a half before the dining-
roon door opened and there frisked in a girl of
eighteen with eyes more bright and shifty than the
waters of Loch Katreen. She was very pretty and
pert; her dress and the ribbons in her hair fluttered
behnd her like the pennons of a prize yacht, and

she held in her arms what I presumed to be the
Irish dog, for he was a pampered beast and the
Scotch and English terriers set up an unhallowed
barking as they sighted him. But Pat O'Coon corrected them with a volley of bread-crusts and sprang
up to dance round the young lady who stood still
staring at me.

"'Tis me own sisther," cried he; "and if ye give
"me sixpence I'll tell ye her name."

This communication was worth more than sixpence. I tendered him a shilling and was assured
that her name was Martha or Pattie; so I advanced,
not without a certain diffidence lest she should let
the Irish dog go, and emitted a hope that she felt
more kindly towards the English nation, of which I
am an ornament, than her near relatives, the
O'Coons, father and son. But at this she flushed
up, and towed a half pound's weight of chesnut
curls off her forehead. "Sure, thin," said she, "we
"belong to a down-throdden nationalitee, as mee
"brother has been tellin' ye, for I was listenin' at
"the kayhole. And, maybe, some day I'll have to
"marry one of ye, if he's a gentleman and rich
"enough; but it'll be self-sacrifice, I assure ye, for
"there's not a man in this counthree can hold a
"candle to the boys in Ireland."

Her impish brother grinned and patted her on

the shoulder; but while I was still standing abashed and observant of the dog, he wheedled five sovereigns out of me by whispering, "Give me five "pounds, ye Inglish spalpeen, to buy gloves for "Pathie, and ye shall kiss her."

It was Pattie herself who pocketed the coins, which I very expeditiously paid out; but when I advanced to complete my part in the welcome bargain, she dropped the Irish dog with the true instinct of national hate between my legs, and fled from the room, laughing. The dog fastened on my calves; and at the same time young Pat O'Coon, ringing the bell, called up the large-eared footman and butler, and some more of them, and sang out, "Here's a base rascal who's bin afther insultin' mee "sisther!"

As the Irish are a chaste people, I was cast out head-long, I believe, and without my stick and hat, which the O'Coon household must have parted among them. As I picked myself out of the road-way, the strains of a piano and the ripples of Miss Pattie's voice purled through the drawing-room window, warbling Moore's most apposite ballad:—

"Blessed for ever is he who relied
On Erin's honour and on Erin's pride."

No. 25.—The Bishop of Wapping's Wife.

MR. GRIPPE, the well-known detective, rented a house in a Lambeth square, and one afternoon whilst he was out looking after some people who were not easy to find, his wife let the first-floor drawing-room and bed-room to a man who had a magpie waiting on the area-railings outside. When asked what his name was, this man answered that he took tea and shaving-water every morning at eight, but that otherwise his name was Ginger, which things having been jotted by Mrs. Grippe on one of her husband's disused paper collars, the new lodger paid down twenty-five shillings in half-crowns, and whistled to the magpie to come in and take possession. An hour later when Mr. Grippe returned home to tea, he perceived Mr. Ginger and the magpie sitting on the sill of an open window, and sharing a round of buttered toast between them; and the magpie forthwith put out her head and screamed at Mr. Grippe, as if the latter were not wanted.

Mr. Grippe came in, however, and having kissed his wife, according to a habit he had acquired when quite a boy, he treated himself to a clean collar, and went up, as courtesy required, to pay his duty to his lodger. Mr. Ginger was six feet high, parted his hair down the middle, had a number of the *Echo* sticking out of his tail pocket, and spoke of the climate of Lambeth as a thing which every man should try who had the means. The magpie tapped her beak on the floor as if she concurred, and Mr. Grippe could get nothing out of them for three months, perhaps because he kept out of their way, being much engaged elsewhere. After three months, however, Mrs. Grippe, who somehow looked keenly after Mr. Ginger's welfare, remarked that there was something wrong in their lodger's hearth-rug, and Mr. Grippe accordingly went up to take note of the damage. The lodger was not changed; he was still six feet high, and he resumed his eulogies of the Lambeth climate at the exact spot where he had left them off. But soon he stopped, for a notable change had come over Mr. Grippe's appearance. Whilom stout and cheery, this detective had become so lean and haggard that the magpie yawned on perceiving him, then hopped under the sofa, and grinned silently at him till the tears ran out of her eyes. As for Mr. Ginger, after a moment's anxious scrutiny of his landlord, as if he wondered whether at this rate there would soon be anything of him left, he laid a hand on Mr. Grippe's shrunken ribs, and said: "Police work doesn't seem to agree with "you."

"No, it don't," answered the Detective, un-grammatically but feelingly; then, glancing at the hearth-rug: "I see what's the matter with that rug—"the magpie has eaten half of it."

. "Yes, the bird has eaten it," replied the Lodger, with a pleasant smile, "but we can arrange the "matter by your taking half-a-crown off my rent. I "covenanted for a whole rug; now that there's only "half a one, it's fair that my payments should be "reduced."

"Perhaps so," replied the Detective, though he stood puzzled for a moment. "Anyhow, I've been "leading such a life that my arithmetic has got con-"fused. Hadn't we better take off five shillings, for "the magpie will finish the rest of the rug, I dare-"say?"

"I think that will be the better arrangement," assented Mr. Ginger, with a nod. "But now may I "inquire who has been making you lead such a "life?"

The Detective cracked his finger-joints, heaved a profound sigh, and wore an expression so desolate

that the magpie hopped from under the sofa, and
gave a succession of little screams indicative of
hysterical amusement. There was something pecu-
liarly inconsiderate in this conduct of the fowl, for
it was evident that Mr. Grippe suffered much in
spirit; and the lodger, feeling ashamed of his bird,
mumbled an apology in her behalf. Mr. Grippe was
partially soothed, and wrung his lodger's hand.

"I feel I can trust you," he said. "For the past
"three months I have been running after a reward
"of £500, offered by the Bishop of Wapping for the
"apprehension of the man who has eloped with his
"wife."

"Dear me, the Bishop's wife has eloped! I have
"heard that he was a most holy man." But as the
Lodger said this, the magpie's conduct grew up-
roarious, for she flapped her wings, and, with shrieks
of laughter, piped, "Holy man! holy man!"

"Yes, the Bishop's wife has eloped," rejoined the
Detective, sliding a surprised glance at the magpie,
"and the man is five foot high, has a hump on his
"back, parts his hair down the side, and reads the
"*Daily Telegraph.*"

"Are those all the clues you have?" inquired
Mr. Ginger, with interest; whereat the magpie, overcome by the comic aspects of the situation, fluttered

on to the window-sill, and screamed hilariously to the people in the square below—"*Clues! Clues!*"

"There is something suspicious in the conduct "of that fowl, and I fancy that her voice is not un- "familiar to me," observed the Detective, gazing again at the bird, but nervously. "As to clues," added he, "the Bishop and his wife lived on the "tenderest terms, but his lordship has confessed to "me that in one of those moments when the tongue "utters a little more than the heart would express, "he requested the companion of his life's labours "to go to Jericho; and I have been asking myself "all this day whether I ought not to proceed to that "city on the chance of finding her there."

"You should certainly go to Jericho," answered the Lodger without a moment's hesitation: "and I'll "tell you what: if the Bishop will pay our expenses "first-class, I will accompany you, and so will the "magpie—three heads being better than one."

"You have forestalled a wish that was rising to my lips," exclaimed Mr. Grippe, with some emotion. "The Bishop will resignedly pay all expenses, for "the disappearance of his wife has excited much "talk in Convocation, and aroused many unsea- "sonable speculations among the lesser clergy. With "respect to the magpie, I have a presentiment that "she will be of use to us."

That same night they all three started for Jericho, Mr. Ginger, Mr. Grippe, and the magpie. They visited every corner of the Holy Land, and went nowhere without a tin of sandwiches and a Hebrew dictionary, to inquire their way when four roads met. Mr. Grippe wore a cork helmet, such as was used to frighten the Ashantees; Mr. Ginger had subscribed for the *Echo* to be sent out to him by post, and, whenever the evenings were sultry, he would read extracts from this light periodical to his two companions seated beside the Brook Kedron, or the Pool of Siloam. It is impossible to imagine a journey conducted under circumstances better calculated to wear out boots and elevate the mind; nevertheless, the pilgrims could find no trace of the Bishop of Wapping's wife, though they sought for her with supplications and shouting. The magpie was set to scream her name in the market place of the Jebusite capital; some children of Gad were hired to wander and yell for her in the suburbs; and a direct descendant of Jubal was provided with a wind instrument wherewith he stirred the echoes of the country round about till the women of Judah stopped their ears and wept, fancying it was the forlorn Bishop himself who was making all this noise. But these things served no purpose, so that after a year and six months the three explorers returned to England, by

way of Bath, pinning their last hope on the chance
of discovering Mrs. Bishop in this English Jericho—
a hope which failed them. Then they took train for
Lambeth, and were received with some mild remonstrances from Mrs. Grippe, who had sorely
missed the company of Mr. Ginger, and who tear-
fully, but innocently, squeezed his fingers while she
was being kissed by her only husband. The next
thing for Mr. Grippe to do was to put on another
clean collar, and to call on the Bishop of Wapping
to explain how vain the pilgrimage had been, and to
beg for a cheque; but as the Detective was starting
on this mixed expedition, Mr. Ginger drew him aside
and whispered: "Tell the Bishop to come here;
"I shall perhaps be able to find something to com-
"fort him."

The Bishop arrived to be comforted. He was a
smooth, sleek prelate, from whose shovel-hat there
radiated infinite benignity on all who approved of
the Public Worship Regulation Bill. His gaiters
were new, his silk apron bent into a dignified con-
vexity at the waist, and his cheeks so resembled a
pair of dimpled peaches that in both Houses of
Convocation it was held as an article of faith that
he had greatly improved since his wife's depar-
ture. But by all, except some rural deans of the
baser sort, this was ascribed to his Christian resignation.

The holy man was shown into the first-floor drawing-room, where the half-eaten hearth-rug still lay. The magpie had been shut up in the adjoining chamber, and when the Bishop entered, Mr. Ginger requested the Detective to leave him in private with his lordship—a demand with which Mr. Grippe complied by crouching on the door-mat outside, and putting his ear professionally to a chink so as not to miss a syllable. But, to outwit this manœuvre, Mr. Ginger addressed the prelate in Greek, a tongue with which all bishops are conversant, though in this instance his lordship took to staring, and finally begged to be spoken to in English, on the plea that he had left his spectacles behind. So pitching his voice in a sweet, low tone, Mr. Ginger repeated in his native dialect:—

"Pray be seated, my lord. They tell me you "have been seeking very anxiously for your wife."

"Very anxiously," moaned the Bishop; "her flight "occasioned much talk in the province of Canter-"bury, and I have had to endure grievous affliction "from the jests of minor canons."

"I would not mind the shots of those little guns," answered Mr. Ginger, quietly gratified by his own joke; "I would rather be of light heart, for it is in "my power to restore to you your wife here in "this room, exactly as she was when you last saw "her."

The good Bishop winced, and his shovel-hat dropped out of his hands. A sudden purple overspread his round features, and he stammered—

"Hem, you are very good; but, of course, if my "Virginia is happier where she is at present, I would "rather not interfere—much rather not! But, God "bless you! it seems to me I have heard or seen you "before?"

"Both, my lord," answered Mr. Ginger sedately. "I am the man five feet high, with the hump on his "back, and who reads the *Daily Telegraph*. Often "called to your palace by motives of business or "pleasure, I was enabled to judge of the state of "bondage in which your wife kept your lordship, and "one day I overheard a fervent, pious wish escape "you that you could be favoured as Lot was."

"Tush, my good sir! 'twas spoken in a moment "of heat," protested the good Bishop, with beads of alarm on his forehead. "I assure you I have re-"pented."

"There was no need to do so," replied Mr. Ginger, with a polite smile. "The wish was very natural in "a holy man who was unversed in the means by "which a too-energetic wife should be brought to "subjection—that is, by——"

"Wapping; Wapping!" screamed a piteous voice from the next room, undoubtedly the magpie's.

"Precisely," continued Mr. Ginger, amused. "I "repeat the wish was so natural that I felt sure it "would be granted, and I had the pleasure of being "the chosen instrument on that occasion, for within "one short hour of your wish I changed Mrs. Bishop "into a magpie."

"My wife a magpie!" exclaimed his lordship, rising to his short legs with uneasy amazement.

"A loquacious magpie of the finest feather," replied Mr. Ginger, proudly. "Yes, my lord, I might "have brought her home to you eighteen months "ago, but I thought a little travelling at your ex- "pense would do us both good; for if there is one "thing I like more than another it is to enjoy "luxuries without paying for them. But now I will "introduce you to Mrs. Bishop, and when you desire, "transform her—chastened, I hope, and softened— "to her original form."

So saying, Mr. Ginger turned the door-handle, and there hopped in the magpie; but not a flaunting magpie with open beak and wings outspread—a humble bird corrected, and craving forgiveness. Meekly, and by reverent jumps, she crossed the carpet, pecked a tender little kiss on the Bishop's shoes, then hopped to his knees. to his shoulder,

and laid her beak against his face. It was a touching sight! The worthy prelate, much moved, rained
tears of emotion over the penitent fowl, while Mr.
Ginger, like a well-bred man, turned away, not to
intrude on the domestic scene. He had been turning away about a quarter of an hour or so, and was
rapping a hymn tune on the window panes in
expectation of being summoned to perform Mrs.
Bishop's metamorphosis, when a stealthy step crept
behind him, and his lordship's hushed voice whispered
pleadingly, "Do you know, my dear sir, I—I think I
"would rather keep her as she is."

Mr. Ginger smiled, closed his left eye admiringly
at the Bishop and clapped him on the shoulder;
and that is why ten minutes later his lordship might
have been seen stepping into his carriage, and hug-
ging with every demonstration of love a wicker cage
with a magpie in it.

And now in the Episcopal palace of Wapping
there is talk only about the affection and care which
the good Bishop bestows on his pet bird. The most
dainty morsels from the dining-room table are reserved for it; the gilt cage where it lives is hung on
a most eligible hook in the sunniest corner of his
lordship's study, and flowers and fruit are brought
it, but no liberty; for on that point the Bishop has
issued his firmest orders that never shall the cage-

door be opened. One of the chaplains—a truthful man —has declared that in passing by his lordship's study he has often heard the Bishop read aloud the sermon he intended delivering on the morrow, and pause now and then as if awaiting praise from the magpie; and another has vouched that such sermon-readings are generally interspersed by fierce screams on the part of the magpie, as if despairing complaints and abuse were being lavished by that spoiled bird. But on such matters let no one trust to hearsay. It must be enough for you and me that there is not a happier or cosier Lord Spiritual at this hour than the Right Reverend Bishop of Wapping.

No. 26.—Marriage not à la Mode.

THE following story should be taken hot with a cup of tea, and if you have no tea by you, please ring for some, and we will both start fair together.

The tea-things being on the table, then, and the urn hissing, as I love to see the public do at the dramas of my literary brethren, Miss Lily, who held the open caddy in her hands, said, "Papa, "I have something very important to ask of you."

"What is it, my dear?" rejoined Mr. Grandsole, uneasily, for he disliked important things, and had been dozing quite contentedly over some blank verses by Mr. Gladstone.

"Papa, I know you are fond of me, and have "always done everything to promote my happi-"ness."

Mr. Grandsole tried to recall when he had done anything to promote the happiness of someone, no matter whom; but not being able to remember the date, replied, placidly, "Yes, my dear."

"Well, papa, mamma wants to make me marry
"Mr. Inkerbus, the engineer," said Lily, with a pout,
"and I had much rather become the wife of Sir
"Mungo Flock, the rich clothier."

Lily closed the caddy with a little bang, turned
the tap of the urn, and when the teapot was full,
came and nestled on to the knees of Mr. Grandsole.
By the same occasion she handed Mr. Gladstone's
verses to her lap-dog, who took and passed them
under the table, recognising them with emotion for
saintly doggerel.

"My dear," stammered Mr. Grandsole, as Lily
affectionately twisted his white hair into a top-knot,
rumpled his shirt-collar, and kissed him. "My dear,
"your mother understands much more about these
"things than you or I."

"But, papa, you don't understand that mamma
"says she is acting for my best interests, and that is
"the aggravating part of it," expostulated Miss Lil.
"She says," 'My pet, Inkerbus is not rich, and his
"humble relations live at Islington; but he is a hand-
"some, strong, and industrious young man, who has
"a great future before him, provided he has a
"loving wife to sustain him in his early struggles,
"and help to bear his sorrows.' Now, papa, I don't
"want to bear any man's sorrows."

"Why not, my dear?"

"Oh, how can you ask? Isn't it much pleasanter
"to be the wife of a man like Sir Mungo, who has a
"town house and a country seat, and will give me a
"box at the opera, and as many new dresses and
"bracelets as I like to ask for? It stands to reason,
"papa, dear."

"I can't contradict you, my love," answered Mr.
Grandsole, with some ruefulness, for he saw that the
dog was underlining the choicest of Mr. Gladstone's
verses with his teeth. "At the same time—but hush!
"I hear your mother coming."

Mrs. Grandsole came in, robed in her mulberry
velvet dress. She had gone upstairs to put it on
after dinner, and, it being ten o'clock, Sir Mungo
Flock and young Mr. Inkerbus soon arrived to spend
the evening. The two gentlemen were very dis-
similar. If you have seen Mr. G. Neville play the
part of a toilsome and sententious young hero in a
high-life comedy by some moralist from the Garrick,
you will get an idea of Mr. Inkerbus. He would
have ridden rough-shod over any number of wretched
peers or money-men in a three-act play, and married
Miss H—— or Miss F—— just before the fall of
the curtain, to the tune of most feeling applause
from the gallery. He could talk about the march of
progress as beautifully as a cheap newspaper. He
had a fine sense of his own mission in life, a healthy

confidence in his own talents, and would have come out nobly as the centre-figure of a home picture by Mr. Frith: Scene, a lodging-house parlour; Mr. Inkerbus drawing plans by the light of a moderator lamp, whilst his pretty wife sat by and darned his socks.

Miserable Sir Mungo had none of these advantages. He was forty and podgy, with no belief in himself at all; just the fellow to have excited the most universal derision at the Globe, the Court, or the Gaiety. But then you should have seen the jewellery he wore. He had a watch with his crest in diamond dust, a ring with a monster ruby in it, and shirt-studs to make your eyes blink. And these blazing gems went straight to the fluttering heart of Miss Lil, so that the pair of lovers had not been in the room five minutes before it became very clear to the meanest observer—or would have been clear had a mean observer been present—with which of the gentlemen her preferences lay.

It was Sir Mungo who got the best cup of tea, with plenty of cream in it. He was made free of all the albums, and allowed to hold the Maltese dog on his lap. When Mr. Inkerbus asked Lily whether she would sing him the songs that he loved, she answered "No," and flouted him quite rudely. But when Sir Mungo put in a claim for a Scotch ballad,

Lily sat down with a smile, and melodiously warbled him one song after another until the clothier's heart inside him was wrung like a big sponge, and brought drops of water into his eyes. The upshot of all this nice play was that towards midnight Mr. Inkerbus went off, gnashing his teeth as Mr. G. Neville does when the banker gets the best of it in the first act, and when he—Mr. Neville—dramatically invokes the Providence which watches over virtuous engineers. When Mr. Inkerbus had levanted, Sir Mungo motioned to Lily with a furtive wag of the head, which that coy maiden understood, and she blushingly left the room. Then, being alone with Mr. and Mrs. Grandsole, lovesick Sir Mungo made a formal proposal for Lily's hand.

"I am so deeply attached to her," he stammered plaintively, "that I don't know whether I am stand-"ing on my head or my heels." Now, he was sitting down when he made the above remark.

"I am sorry you should be in such a plight, Sir "Mungo," answered Mrs. Grandsole, with severity; "but I cannot approve of your attachment, and must "ask you to discontinue your visits. Mr. Grandsole "and I are responsible for our child's happiness, "and we can never give her to a man who would "not maintain her in the style suited to her posi-"tion."

"But I will settle five thousand a year on her; "she shall have two carriages and six horses," pleaded the rich clothier.

"You misunderstand me, Sir Mungo," answered Mrs. Grandsole, with some pity. "Riches do not "make happiness, and the proper lot of young "girls is to be the wives of poor but laborious "men."

"Those are novel sentiments," submitted wretched Sir Mungo, who had heard nothing like them in the City.

"They are sentiments I have found in all good "novels, and also on the stages of such theatres as I "frequent—and I frequent none but good theatres, "Sir Mungo," said Mrs. Grandsole, with quiet self-complacency. "The best literature of our day teems "with examples of the misfortunes which result from "ill-assorted unions between beautiful girls and too "rich suitors. Heaven preserve my Lily from in-"curring such misfortunes!"

"But it's not my fault if I'm rich," expostulated the clothier, in thorough despondency.

"I do not say it is, and, believe me, I am far "from seeking to reproach you, Sir Mungo," replied Mrs. Grandsole, not unkindly; "but I beg you to "consider the position of a mother. In our times, "Sir Mungo, the best education that can be given

"to a girl is surely that which teaches her to sew
"our shirt-buttons, to check the butcher's account,
"aye, and to busy herself in the kitchen and roll a
"pudding with her own hands. I read an edifying
"article on that subject in some Liberal periodical
"no earlier than last week."

"Her little hands were never, never made to roll
"roley-poley puddings," protested honest Sir Mungo,
who had a great deal of poetry in his composition.

But this lyrical flight did not save him. He was
too rich to mate fitly with a girl whose path had
been traced in the sphere of life where imposing
heroes like Mr. Inkerbus shed their effulgence. Mr.
Grandsole, who was touched by his dejection, did
indeed put in a word for him; but motherly Mrs.
Grandsole was not to be wiled from the track of
duty. Judged by the canons laid down for us in
the refreshing popular prints and plays, Sir Mungo
Flock had been tried and found wanting. So Miss
Lily, who had been lurking behind the hat-stand in
the hall, saw him go out punching his be-ringed
fists into his eyes to keep the tears from flowing,
and she had only time to blow him a despairing
kiss of sympathy and faithfulness when the hand of
a mother was laid on her shoulder and brought her
resolutely back to propriety and the drawing-room.

Now, miss, what should you do if your mamma

prevented you from marrying a rich City man who offered you large settlements, diamond necklaces, an opera-box, and the rest? I am sorry to say Miss Lily took the very improper and undutiful course of corresponding privately with Sir Mungo. The housemaid was the intermediary who carried letters to the persistent clothier, received others back, and was paid for her services with bank notes. And so it came to pass that Mrs. Grandsole continuing inexorable, Mr. Grandsole weak, and Mr. Inkerbus importunate, an old, old story was repeated. One morning after breakfast Miss Lily disappeared under the pretence that she was going out shopping, and the same day at eleven she was secretly married at St. George's. She has been Lady Flock ever since, and her dresses, horses, tiaras, and grand-tier box, excited much admiration last season. I wish I could add that her wicked conduct had been visited upon her with the consequences that point the morals of all good books; but a pound of truth is worth a world of fiction, and I am bound to state that Lily and Sir Mungo make a very happy pair. You will say what next? but I don't know.

No. 27.—Honesty and Happiness.

A KIND father having three bright sons begged them one day to choose each a profession. The first two made satisfactory selections; but the third, a thoughtful boy, of whom great things were expected, answered, pleadingly, "Father, I should like to be a "thief."

The father smiled. His thoughtful son must have got this notion out of the adventures of Dick Turpin or Jack Sheppard, two fine characters as sketched by Mr. Ainsworth; but, anyhow, the reply betrayed a consciousness of vocation which it would have been unwise to ignore. The prudent parent probes the capacities of his offspring, and directs them in a channel where they may best redound to the offspring's advantage. So did this prudent parent, who answered, "Robert, I shall place you "in the office of my old friend, Mr. Farrissey, of "Manchester, a prosperous and much respected man, "as you will find."

Robert cared little for the respectability of Mr. Farrissey, but hearing that this gentleman possessed a fine place in the country, a poultry yard, an orchard, a picture gallery, and a cabinet of saleable curiosities, he was pleased, and started for his new home with hopeful anticipations. He arrived at Manchester late in the evening, and reached Mr. Farrissey's house just in time to partake of a supper-tea, after which he was regaled with family prayers and a chapter of the Bible, which Mr. Farrissey roared to his assembled domestics with a heartiness which brought the perspiration to his brow. Mrs. Farrissey listened unctuously with folded hands, and said "Amen" at the prayer-responses; and Miss Olive Farrissey sat with her legs tucked up under a chair, and pulled faces at Robert when she could do so unobserved.

Robert was then twelve years old, and Olive nine; Mrs. Farrissey was scarcely thirty, and Mr. Farrissey dyed his hair and whiskers so that there was no guessing his age with accuracy. They were a remarkably pious household. Mr. and Mrs. Farrissey frequently sighed over the sinfulness of this world of ours; and it would have been difficult to find a couple more continually on the look-out to detect the blemishes of their neighbours. If there was an ambiguous passage in a book Mrs. Farrissey ran as straight to it as a certain nameless animal does to a truffle bed, and she would order the unclean book out of the house with gestures of disgust quite impressive; if there was a loose sentiment or a too light joke in a newspaper, Mr. Farrissey exclaimed in dismay and wrote a Scriptural homily to the editor. Both Farrisseys had been known to leave a theatre in a noisy manner because a lighthearted young lady on the stage had pointed her satin shoe towards the chandelier, and they had declared that a certain fine-art exhibition was a most improper sight, because of some mediæval statue which stood up unblushingly without a fig-leaf. It is a comfort to add that Mr. and Mrs. Farrissey professed to guide their conduct entirely by Holy Writ, and could cite Biblical precedents to justify the courses they took in even the smallest contingencies of life. For instance, they were inclined to limit their charities to doles of twopence because the Good Samaritan has been immortalised by that sum, and they only relaxed their rule when the charities could be printed in the public papers, on which occasions they would talk of not hiding their lights under a bushel, and draw comfort from the text, "He that giveth plenteously shall reap "plenteously." They would have made conscientious reapers the pair of them.

Now Robert, who had come to Farrissey Hall with the hope that he should be able to indulge his propensities towards misappropriation, was not over delighted when he discovered the shining virtues of his hosts. He had counted that Mr. Farrissey would be a jovial fellow, who might teach him to ride and shoot, and rig him out in time for the free life of a bush-ranger; but the very first lesson inculcated upon him by that gentleman was that Honesty is the royal road to happiness. Robert was naturally too young to start on this road by being admitted into Mr. Farrissey's counting-house, so it had been arranged that he should have a tutor to give him lessons every day, and in the evenings profit by Mr. Farrissey's kind instructions in book-keeping with a view to becoming eventually his religious patron's partner. Mr. Farrissey forthwith provided him with a tutor at once evangelical and stern; and he himself in imparting his hints as to book-keeping interlarded them with sanctimonious phrases of the sort used to embellish copybooks. But when Robert perceived these things he felt duped, and as a letter of remonstrance which he forwarded to his father only evoked a reply that he should be an obedient lad, he began to brew schemes for making away with some of Mr. Farrissey's valuable curiosities and setting up in life for himself. But he was deterred by a discovery which gave him to reflect that there might after all be some means of coming to an understanding with his hosts.

The thing came about in this way: Mr. Farrissey having announced one night that he was going to attend a meeting for the propagation of Dr. Watts' hymns in foreign parts went out in evening clothes; and soon afterwards Robert, who had a ticket for some magic-lantern show in Manchester, sallied forth too. Robert, however, had little taste for magic-lanterns, and was accordingly wending his furtive way to a music-hall when whom should he see alighting at a coquettish house near the Theatre Royal but Mr. Farrissey carefully muffled but still recognisable. A postman came by soon afterwards, and Robert, already an acute boy, extracted from him by means of a two-shilling bit that the tenant of the house in question was Miss Bella Jigge—an actress, and the very young lady by the way whose pedal feat had once caused Mr. and Mrs. Farrissey to run from the theatre in horror. Robert waited a couple of hours, and then saw Mr. Farrissey emerge from the house, at the same time a window opened on the first floor, and a fair form leaned out to blow the retreating visitor a kiss. Chuckling somewhat over his adventure, Robert re-

turned home and related his magic-lantern ex-
periences with a graphic minuteness, only equalled
by Mr. Farrissey's zest in expatiating on the hymns
he had been singing all the evening.

But from that day Robert began of-times to absent himself of an evening, under pretext of attending places of worship, and the gratification of the
Farrisseys was great thereat; till one night Mr. Farrissey, returning from another visit to Miss Jigge's,
stumbled right upon Robert issuing from a theatre
where operettas were performed. The consequences
of this encounter were in the highest degree unpleasant. Mr. Farrissey had well laid to heart the lesson about spoiling the rod for the good of the
child, and he owned a riding-whip, which, on arriving home, he laid across Robert's back, till it was
bent like a broken reed. "Well, but how about
"Miss Jigge?" yelped the boy, under the torture of
the infliction. "I'll tell Mrs. Farrissey—so you'd
"better look out."

"Ah! calumny allied to dissimulation and de-
"bauchery!" raved Mr. Farrissey; and the stripes fell
again in such a shower, that Robert's inclination
to denounce his benefactor was soon perfectly thrashed
out of him.

The flogging was indeed severe—too thoroughly
so to be lightly forgotten; and for a time Robert

directed all his energies towards escaping a renewal
of it. Some months later, however, being on a visit
to Mr. Farrissey's store-house, he was left alone for
a few minutes with some piles of cotton, which were
to be made up in bales for foreign exportation, the
bales in question being all marked "Quality A. 1."
Robert was of an inquiring turn of mind, so he took
some of the cotton flocks in his hand, and, softly
rubbing them between his finger and thumb, became
aware that they were filled with clay. "Is cotton
"sold by the weight?" he asked, innocently, of a
packer, who entered just then. "Yes, sir," grinned
the man; and his reply was like a seed falling on
well ploughed land.

Very well ploughed, for Robert was allowed by
Mr. Farrissey to sell to the cook the eggs of half-a-
dozen hens, which had been given him to develop
his taste for harmless pursuits. Unfortunately, these
fowls did not lay with the regularity desirable; but
after Robert's visit to the store-house it was noticed
that his hens furnished six eggs punctually every
morning, in fair weather or foul. They did so for
a week or so, but, at the end of this time, the cook,
going deep into the matter, ascertained that the eggs
were addled; whereon a watch was set upon Robert,
and he was descried selling his good eggs for three
halfpence a-piece to a dairy-woman, and purchasing

of her, at the rate of a penny the half-dozen, addled eggs which were to be retailed to the cook. This led to his being summoned once more to Mr. Farrissey's study, and that gentleman took down the riding-whip. "Well, but how about your clayed cotton?" howled Robert, as the first blow whistled through the air upon his shoulders. "I'll write to your con-"signees, you see if I don't!"

"Ah, cynicism allied to dishonesty of the grossest "sort!" shouted Mr. Farrissey; and for the next few minutes the study resounded with weals and appalling howls.

But this was the last chastisement. From that day forth Robert learned the wisdom of honesty, and practised it. Having caught Mrs. Farrissey slipping a note into the hand of a dragoon officer he closed his eyes to the fact; and by-and-bye, when he entered the Farrissey counting-house, and detected that two and two made three or five according to circumstances in the accounts of the firm, he feigned to be unconscious of this also; and by this means throve more and more in the favour of his employers. One need not follow him on his prosperous career. He married Olive Farrissey, became a great man in Manchester, a knight, and a Liberal M.P. When he has time to spare of an evening he sings hymns as his father-in-law did, and the cotton of his firm still outweighs that of all competitors in the scales of foreign nations. Please the Fates, he will end by being a Peer like X. Y. and Z., whom we all of us know. But meanwhile Mr. Farrissey often says to him in the free-and-easy hour of port, "Do you re-"member what a dishonest little chap you used to "be, Robert? Where should you have been now if I "hadn't corrected you?"

"Where, indeed?" answers Robert, feelingly. "Being a magistrate I can see by the example of the "poor thieves whom I send to prison whither dis-"honest courses lead."

And they both smile pensively.

No. 28.—The Goose Quill.

EVER since I discovered that I could earn three halfpence a column daily comfortably by stringing sentences on paper I began to wish for the pen of a ready writer. Not an ordinary pen that would only go when driven, but one that would run ahead on its own responsibility, like a steeple-chaser with a Frenchman in the saddle. I have had opportunities for noticing that when I wish for a thing it sometimes comes to pass and sometimes does not; and in the present case, being minded to find an instrument that should do what no instrument ever did before, I had a sort of notion that my ambition would not be gratified. It was then I remembered what a valuable present of a Yellow Dog* had been made me by the Girl with the Mocking Eyes. She had in truth flung me three times into the water before making her gift; but I forgave her in consideration of her motives, which were sincere; and I thought it might be worth while taking three more baths with my clothes on for the sake of obtaining a pen which

* See No. 4. p. 30.

should make me earn bread-and-cheese and public admiration for the remainder of my days. He who learns to act thus dispassionately on his private affairs will find money accumulate in his pockets like dust on the prayer-books of some public men of my acquaintance.

I accordingly repaired to the Tell-Tale-Torrent, and found it in the same place as before. There was the site where the Girl had reclined on the moss-bank; there the ledge of rock whence she had pitched me into the waters by means of cuffs on the ears; and, opposite, the spot where the Boy had knelt, throwing stones at the frogs. But the Girl was absent; and it was only by groping on all fours over some sharp stones and a puddle or two that I reached a pine tree, on which was nailed this notice:—

ALL APPLICATIONS TO THE

GIRL WITH THE MOCKING EYES

TO BE MADE IN WRITING, AND TO
BE WRITTEN ON ONE SIDE ONLY OF THE PAPER.

NO ATTENTION WILL BE PAID TO THEM.

---

*She has gone away to the GOOSE FIELDS as far
in front of you as you can walk.*

As far in front of me as I could walk was a vague term, for, like most of you, I could have walked a day and a night to escape my creditors and scarcely a mile to reach a sermon; but splitting the difference, as it were, I cleared an uncertain number of miles and found myself in the Goose Fields at the hour when, judging by appearances, the geese practised for chorus-singing. There might have been seen a thousand geese or two strewn over the locality; and in a corner of the field on a hedge-bank overshadowed by an arbour of honeysuckle and white roses sat the Girl with the Mocking Eyes, staring saucily to see what business had brought me hither.

She was dressed in black velvet with coral bracelets round her wrists, and was eating scarlet cherries. I approached with politeness, and noticing that she had grown a little plumper and staider since our last meetings, concluded she had got married, and told her so.

"Married; oh, how absurd!" she laughed. "What "should I want husbands for?"

"The singular of that noun would be more "proper than the plural on the lips of a young "person like you," I answered with some severity, and then I proceeded to detail the object of my visit.

"Ah, you men are all the same," she exclaimed,

as she listened. "What have you done with the "Yellow Dog?"

"I made a present of him to Mr. ——," I said, mentioning the name of an esteemed politician. "And "in the society of that great man who never tells "lies he gets on capitally, having no cause to howl."

"What next," she tittered, with a shrug; "will "you have some cherries?"

"That depends whether you will give me any."

"I never had the remotest idea of so doing," was her reply, "but I will give you a goose-quill. "Here, Jimmy!"

The personage addressed as Jimmy was a gray and white goose, who waddled forward at the summons, and cocked his head on one side to examine me. What an old goose he was, and what a depth of inquiry there was in the golden eye which he bent first on my boots, then successively on other portions of my attire till he reached the crown of my head! Hundreds of other geese clustered behind him, forming an excited circle, laying their heads together, and seeming to giggle as though in the event of an encounter of wits between Jimmy and me they would back their friend for any small sum I pleased to name. "Here, Jimmy," said the Girl, in her musical voice, "give the gentleman a "quill, there's a good bird."

But hereat an uproar arose. All the geese flapped their wings and cackled as though nothing in my attitude had prepared them for this communication; and Jimmy himself danced about from foot to foot as if an unjust advantage was being taken of him. The girl was obliged to catch up a bundle of peacock's feathers, and wave it over the heads of the flock, whereupon they dispersed in a hurry; and Jimmy, in his unmartial eagerness to be foremost in the flight, dropped from under his left wing a fine white quill at least twenty inches long. The girl ran forward and picked it up.

"Here's a fine pen," said she, smoothing the feathers with her fingers, "and you see how un-"willing that bird was to part with it; for they all "sell their quills in the market at Poldeedy, and the "profits are equally divided among them, everything "here being done by co-operation."

"Where is Poldeedy?" I asked.

"Never mind where Poldeedy is, but this quill "comes from the bird's left side, where his great "heart lies, and it is white—symbol of purity. "I don't know whether your thoughts are pure, "but as you complained that you had a dif-"ficulty in expressing them fluently on paper, here "is a pen that will enable you to write everything "that may be on your mind. You will only have

"to sit down and let the pen run. Your style will
"be terse and brilliant, your views luminous, and
"your wit pungent; but recollect you will only be able
"to write things which you conscientiously believe."

"I should under no conceivable circumstances
"be tempted to write others," I answered, displeased
by the inuendo.

"That is an untruth," said she, coolly biting a
cherry, and having removed the stone, she squeezed
it between her fingers so that it flew into my face
and stung me. "Take that and your pen and be-
"gone," she added, pertly, "and remember that if
"you get tired of the pen you can send it me back
"by letter postage, paid; and if the whim is on
"me I may perhaps forward you another—there's no
"knowing what I may do when the whim is on me."

"Last time you boxed my ears," I remarked,
"are you going to do the same to-day?"

"I will with pleasure if you like," said she, making a fold in her dress to hold her cherries, and so
getting her right hand free; but seeing me recede
her eyes sparkled mockingly, and she ejaculated,
"No, you're not worth running after; but the geese
"shall escort you out of the field."

Saying this she waved her peacock's feathers,
and the geese, hastening up in swarms, hissing,
cackling, and treading on one another's yellow feet,

spread themselves into two long rows, making a lane through which I had to pass. From my first step to my last they treated me abominably. Some of them pecked at my legs, others flew upwards and bumped me in the back, while Jimmy and two more who seemed to be his best friends, skurried in front, and kicked up clouds of dust and pebbles into my eyes. I began to run, but they doubled after me, and it was not till I had cleared a hedge and ditch at the end of the field, and landed myself amid some wet turnips that I was at last rid of the brutes. They stood grouped in legions, craning their necks over the hedge-bank, and crying "H-s-s-s-s" to me; and I, wiping the dust off my eyes with one hand, clenched the other at them, and bawled, "Boh! you "ugly lot, I'll be even with you at Michaelmas!"

I had my pen though—and yet alack! no sooner was I home than I sat down to try this bountiful quill, which was to render me at once fluent and luminous, pungent and conscientious, and I discovered with some surprise (for I was used to puff wares) that it far more than fulfilled my expectations. Its gliding over the paper was beautifully smooth, serene, and spontaneous; substantives and verbs, vigorous interjections, and lusty adjectives arrayed themselves in order like the lines of a battalion, and by day-break, after a dozen hours or so of fatigue-less, nay voluptuous, writing I had composed this attractive lot of copy:— 1. An article on a social subject; 2. a political leader about the Irish; 3. a Positivist essay, the most erudite yet penned; 4. a thrilling narrative of adventure; 5. the first chapter of a popular novel.

Greatly esteeming myself after this feat, presumably unparalleled, I washed my face, took some drink, and then a cab, which deposited me and my basket (for I had put the MSS. into a basket to avoid crumpling) at the door of an able editor, who passed most of the small hours measuring out philosophy and other things in demand by the column.

"Here, Tungo!" I shouted, embracing him like a brother; "here's an assortment for you and you shall "choose!"

He chose nothing. Taking up the compositions one by one he yelled over the humour, wit, terseness, pathos, breadth of perception, &c., in them like a Choctaw sighting a scalp. He was transported, bewildered, here and there moved to snivelling, and in fact he became my ardent admirer from that morning at a quarter to eleven. "But, but," cried he as he shovelled the whole lot into the basket again, and pressed down the lid with his shoe; "what in the name of Old Nick am I to do with "writing of that sort?"

"Print some of it!" I holloaed.

"Never," howled he, catching up a ruler in self-defence. "You've said that there are plenty of "minxes to be found in Dorcas clubs, that there are "donkeys in Downing Street, that the Irish ought to "be bambooed, and that the Royal Family were once "tadpoles like the rest of us. I'm not going to "publish those things."

"But they're my conscientious beliefs!" I sang out, shaking a Post Office Directory in his face.

"I don't care a brass shilling for your conscien-"tious beliefs. Get out!" he yelped; and calling in desperate whoops, like an unmannerly cur as he was, for some printers' devils and a man with a paper cap and inky arms, he had me shown into the street by some short way which I had not time to notice.

I daresay you would like to hear how I fared going on a tour of visits to other editors, but I am not going to tell you. My basket had a hole in it before the week was out, and I found that some bunches of my hair were missing in places where I had been accustomed to find them regularly of a morning. I say nothing of my hoarseness, nor of my hat which was lost in Fleet Street, nor of the skirts of my coat which disappeared in different places where I cannot recollect. The upshot of all this was that towards the end of a week my goose-quill went back by registered parcel to the Girl with the Mocking Eyes; and post for post I received another —gray this time—with a laconic note intimating that this new pen would only serve me to write things in which I had no sort of belief whatever.

I prefer my gray quill to my white one. I am rich now, and have a great reputation in the literary market. Tungo has forgiven me for helping me downstairs, and lets me fill his columns with disquisitions which he and I and our readers and everybody else know to be fustian, but which sell mighty well for all that on the knife-boards of 'busses and in other high places. I have forgotten the very name of the implement with which one goes digging, so great is my care not to offend people, and if I had room here I would quote you a few of my leaders at length that you might judge for yourselves what an art there is in eking out nothing into hundreds of words. But you probably take in many of my compositions at breakfast with your other buttered food, so I have nothing further to add for the present except that any of you may send me some presents of game or fruit if you please.

THE END.

PRINTING OFFICE OF THE PUBLISHER.